W I T H D R A W N

WORN, SOILED, OBSOLETE

going under

Also by **Kathe Koja**

straydog
Buddha Boy
The Blue Mirror
Talk

going under

kathe koja

FRANCES FOSTER BOOKS

FARRAR, STRAUS and GIROUX

NEW YORK

Distributed in Canada by Douglas & McIntyre Ltd.
Printed and bound in the United States of America
Designed by Barbara Grzeslo
First edition, 2006
1   3   5   7   9   10   8   6   4   2

www.fsgkidsbooks.com

Library of Congress Cataloging-in-Publication Data
Koja, Kathe.
    Going under / Kathe Koja.— 1st ed.
        p.   cm.
    Summary: Alternating passages that draw on the myths of Persephone
and Narcissus juxtapose the differing viewpoints of a teenaged girl and
her older brother as she tries to prevent a manipulative psychotherapist
from using her journal as material in a book.
    ISBN-13: 978-0-374-30393-8
    ISBN-10: 0-374-30393-2
    [1. Self-perception—Fiction.   2. Brothers and sisters—Fiction.
3. Emotional problems—Fiction.   4. Psychotherapy—Fiction.
5. Diaries—Fiction.]   I. Title.

PZ7.K8312Are 2006
[Fic]—dc22

                                                    2005047711

My thanks to Amy Ryberg, Gwen Braude, Rick Lieder,
Aaron Mustamaa, Frances Foster, Janine O'Malley,
and Chris Schelling

To Chris, my accompanist

going under

1

IN THE CAR, A COLD DRIZZLE SLIPPERY ON THE ROAD, slush backwash but I don't care, I know how to drive, I've been driving since I was fourteen. In the backseat, Marshall and Ada, their worried static mutter back and forth: *doctor* and *seems to* and *will she?* She meaning Hilly who hunches in the seat beside me, long knees up like some cartoon spider, parka hood tugged low like a carapace, a stained, iridescent blue; forget it, Spooky. You know I can see you.

"Change the station," she says.

I flip it randomly from XRZ to classical, news, weather, top 40, that dumb commercial for Telly's Deli, *light lunchtime fare with downtown flair*—

"Ten percent off if you find a hair—"

"Twenty," Hilly's murmur, "if it's a rat hair."

"Fifty if it's a pube."

"Ivan," Marshall, pained, "please."

"Hilly?" Ada leans forward, trying to sound casual. As if she could. As if she ever is. "How are you liking Dr. Molloy?"

Rain in silver zigzags down the windshield. Hilly shifts

in the seat; now I see her face, two bright straight lines: tears. Her voice is normal. "He's OK, I guess."

"No he's not," I say as I palm the wheel, making the long loop onto westbound Oak. Bare March trees, empty car wash, Elder's Wine Shoppe with its painted grapes. I cut off a dark green Jeep. "He's an idiot. An idiot in a corduroy blazer."

"Ivan," Marshall right behind my head, "really, you're not being fair—"

"Fair? Do you know what he wants her to do? *Collage her feelings*. With *Teen People* and a glue stick. Jesus. Give me the money, I'll be her shrink—"

"Ivan, please, that's enough."

Hilly turns her face toward the window, shoulders hunched tight, so I stop talking, turn the radio up, lite syrup jazz all the way to our driveway. Hilly's out before the car stops rolling, loping into the backyard, way back to where our fort used to be; Ada tries to follow but "Let her go," I say, hand on her arm, rain down my neck. Marshall passes us, head down, into the house. "She doesn't want you now."

"Ivan, she's crying, she— And it's *raining*." Mouth all pinched, she's going to cry next. "She'll get wet."

"She'll dry off. . . . Ada. Mom. Come on," as I lead her inside to the kitchen, leave her with Marshall making coffee, and go up to my room where from the window I can see Hilly, arms hooked around her knees, head turtled into her hood: pure concentration. Like a Zen statue. Or a cluster bomb.

She stays out there until it's dark. She gets wet.

See, they mean well, Marshall and Ada, Daddy and Mummy. They're not stupid, they read all the books, they try to do their best. But they get scared easily, they hear *refractive trauma* and *teenage suicide* and they start manning the lifeboats, they think that because Hilly's pal at *High Tide*— or *Riptide* or *Currents* or whatever that stupid literary magazine calls itself—just because Elisha jumped off the gym roof, Hilly's going to do it, too. Just because Hilly cries, and won't sleep in her room anymore. So what? I told them. Hilly's smart, she'll figure things out on her own, and anyway I can help her. Besides, isn't it really their fault in the first place for letting her go to the high school? I mean why does Marshall work overtime at the sports clinic so Ada can be Mrs. Homeschool, if they end up caving in and letting Hilly hang out with monosyllabic cheerleaders at Dumbass High?

OK, so maybe Marshall's got a partial point, I'm not being "fair." Elisha wasn't actually a cheerleader, and there was no real reason, other than that it's kind of stupid, for Hilly not to be on the magazine staff. Hilly and I had had some talks about it before she joined. Mostly I talked and she listened: about how this whole in-school/not-of-school business was bogus to start with, and how the magazine was clearly an inferior product, with some dumb teacher for an adviser and a fascist senior editor who'd read maybe one-tenth as much in her whole life as Hilly had last year. But if Hilly wanted to spend three afternoons a week at Jarvis, watching people argue and sneak smokes and try to hook up, why not? It wasn't like she could be doing something more useful with her time, like driving into the city with me, or finishing her research thing for Ada, or writing in her journal, real writing, not vampire poems or tales of TV true romance—

Come on. That's not what Currents is.

I've read it, Hilly, I—

You read half of one issue.

You don't need to eat a whole bag of shit to know it's shitty.

I don't care. It's fun to do layout. And besides, they're really nice, Elisha and Kim—

Nice like what? Stuffed baby chicks? Circus peanuts? A big warm mug of flat ginger ale? but by then she was giving me that look, her carved-in-stone Easter Island look, she just wasn't going to listen anymore so fine, let her go absorb teen culture or whatever. I was into this big Shards of Evil tournament online at the time, and Marshall was after me to think about college, or at least think about thinking about college: You've had your certificate for over a year now, Ivan, don't you think you really ought to—

I learn by living. By "experience," isn't that what you're always saying? That experience is what matters?

Yes, of course. Absolutely. But you also need to consider your future—

The future is Tuesday, Marshall.

But when I heard about Elisha's dry dive I wasn't really, you know, prepared for it, or for Hilly kind of falling apart—well not apart, but the crying and, and everything.

So when Marshall and Ada consulted the school shi think about it: how bad a shrink do you have to be, working in a high school? even a quote-unquote magnet school like Jarvis?—I wasn't totally on top of things; the guy saw Hilly like twice before I even knew it was happening. I guess all the lit mag kids went there after the funeral, for grief counseling or something, and some of them just kept on going.

But then Mr. School Shrink sees that he can't begin to measure up to Hilly, naturally, she should have been counseling *him*, so he passes the buck—*developmental issues, depression*, I read the letter—and refers her where? To Corduroy Molloy and his *Teen People*. No wonder Hilly sits out in the fucking yard.

Where she is now, again, in the watery morning sun, cross-legged by our ex-fort on a crumpled-up blue tarp, picking at the yellowed winter grass. The fort's long gone but you can still see the little slope we made, all the way back to the fence, so the water would run down and away and keep our fort floor from turning into mud. Smart little bastards, huh? We still are.

"Hey." As I walk up, keys in hand, I can't tell if she's crying or what; she's wearing Marshall's old sunglasses and a baseball cap, her dreads, braids, draids, whatever she calls them, bunched and sticking out the back. An old leaf clings damp to her jacket; I flick it off. "Were you out here all night?"

"No." Picking at the grass, dead blade, dead blade, she

picks a live one by mistake, and sighs. "Where are you going?"

"To get cigarettes. You want to take a ride?"

"No."

"Come on. You can even drive. You still need to get hours for your license—"

"I don't want my license."

"Don't want your license, don't want to sleep in your bed—why don't you sleep in your bed, by the way?"

"Too much like a coffin."

"Liar. Save it for the shrinks," which makes her smile, a genuine smile, the first one I've seen in weeks. Then "I can't . . . think in the house," she says. "Out here is better."

"No house," lighting the last of my cigarettes, "no driving, no writing, what do you want to do?" but before she can get all Easter Island on me "Hilly," I say, "come on. You know you have to write about it. Sooner or later."

She tilts her head away, faint sun on the warped sunglasses. She doesn't answer.

"You don't have to show me or anything. But you need to get it down—"

"No," so low I almost don't hear but I do, and anyway I knew she was going to say it, she's been saying it for months now, two months of no journal, none at all. How do I know? I looked. Hey, if she really didn't want me to read it she'd hide it better; she knows me, OK? And there's nothing there, just some old stuff about the magazine's spring issue, so-and-so said blah-blah-blah, nothing crucial. Then silence, the blank page. The shrinks don't know about that, or Marshall and Ada either. But I do.

"Come on," I say. "You have to write about it, how can you not? This is like a rite-of-passage thing, this is life and death—"

"Stop it." She picks more grass, digs her fingers in. *If you want me again look for me under your boot-soles:* Walt Whitman, leaves of dead grass, tears leaking now from under the sunglasses, shiny lines like slug tracks. Worms, underground. "Don't talk about that, you don't understand—"

"Understand what? That you waste your time humoring them," nodding back at the house, where Ada's no doubt peering out the window, wringing her hands, "going to that moron Molloy, when you could get better in a weekend just by writing it all down, you could—Hilly— aw, Spooky, don't. Don't," but now she's shutting down, arms locked around her legs, head into the parka hood, closing *the valves of her attention,* Emily Dickinson, I read too much fucking poetry, I don't know what else to say—

—so I walk away, drive away, get all the way to the convenience store on Maple Road where the fat guy in the Winstons T-shirt doesn't want to sell me cigarettes, am I eighteen? so I say of course I am, handing over my fake state ID that's good enough for him, or for the security cameras anyway. So out I go, lighting up, aiming home—

—but I don't want to go home, I don't *like* seeing Hilly cry, I don't know exactly what to do about it. Which makes me fucking *cranky.* . . . You might think it's our parents' problem, obligation, whatever, that Marshall and Ada ought to be out there in the backyard trying to deal with her, get her back in the house, get her better. But like I said, they mean well. Which in the end means nothing at all.

As usual, the whole thing's up to me.

2

O<small>H, IVAN.</small>

It wasn't your fault, not all of it; I know. And you never meant to hurt me, ever, you just—wanted what you wanted. As usual.

And some things you were right about. Like about the crying. A lot of it, most of it *was* for Elisha, but that was normal, that was right. Like a cut that needs to bleed before it heals. I tried once or twice to tell you how sad it was, and how I just kept thinking of her, seeing her again and again in my mind's eye: all alone on the roof at Jarvis, stepping out of her shoes, her black-cat sneakers, there by the boiler vent. A car or two goes by below, she steps to the edge of the edge. . . . Was it windy, up there? Was it cold? Did she cry?

Just two nights before, that Tuesday we stayed so late, she sat beside me at the computer, doing cut-and-paste and Hills, she said. *If I was gone, would you miss me?*

Of course I would miss you. Bluish light on her white skin, on my fingers poised at the keyboard. *Why? Are you going somewhere?*

And she just smiled; she leaned her head against mine

for a second, and smiled. Warm red hair against my cheek, her cherry-lipstick smell, and then on Thursday—

Mrs. Price was the one who told me, she called me at home. And then Kim called, I could hardly understand her, she could hardly talk. And all I could think, over and over, was Why didn't I ask Elisha more, push for an answer, was there something I could have done to make her stop? When she said "gone," I just thought—I don't know, that she might quit Currents, or something. It sounds ridiculous but that's what I thought, I never ever in a million years—

—but that's what I mean, that's why I cried so hard. Because I didn't know, I couldn't see, even though we were friends I hadn't seen her.

Like you couldn't see me.

It was like I had always been transparent, even to myself, but now I was slowly turning . . . opaque. Like everything I was was swirling, settling, very slowly turning solid inside. But you didn't see that, you just kept looking on the surface, pilot to copilot, seeing just what I had always been: your little sister, Spooky, with her pencil and notebook, her peace-bead necklace and dangling draids. Someone to tag along behind you, someone to admire you, someone you could boss around.

You didn't see me writing either, so you thought that was the problem. But I know you read my journal, you've been reading it for years, forever. So I started writing one that you didn't know about, out there in the backyard, under the blue tarp. You hate to sit outside; I knew I was safe there.

"Safe." From you. . . . Oh, God. It's not that I wanted to get away from you, Ivan, or leave you behind; never. I just wanted to be—myself.

Marshall and Ada always talked about experience being the best teacher, how we learn the most not from what we're told, but from what we do. Now I know experience is a muscle. Or a scar. Or both.

But you were right that I had to write it down. All of it. And I did.

3

"WHY ARE YOU HERE?" SHE SAYS AS WE CROSS
the parking lot, blacktop and concrete planters, then says
it again as we sit down: tapioca beige chairs, crappy land-
scape print, *Real Time* and *Style Now!* scattered on the tables
and "It's a waiting room," I say. "Right? So I'm waiting."

She gives me a look, sighs, starts gnawing at her thumb-
nail; the skin's all red and ragged there, it looks sick.

"Hilly. Stop."

She scowls, tucks her hand under her thigh. I'm the
only one who can make her stop, make her do anything
that she doesn't want to do. It's always been that way, ever
since she was tiny: *Pilot to copilot,* I'd say. *Go get us some cook-
ies,* or whatever. And she'd say *Copilot to pilot!* and do it. In
my wallet there's a picture of us in swimsuits on the
beach, we're like four and two. Sun hats, pails and shovels,
I'm looking at the camera, but Hilly's looking up at me.
. . . I couldn't really pronounce "Hillary" when she was
born, so I called her "Hilly." And it stuck. So I'm the one
who named her, really. No one ever calls her Hillary.

When Hilly was born, Marshall and Ada kind of gave
up, or in, or whatever. I mean, you have one kid who's

very smart, he's teaching himself to read by age two, he's way more than you can handle—and then you go and have *another* one. They did Montessori and museums and Baby-Play-By-Numbers, all the stuff you do with little brainiacs, but pretty quickly they figured out who was in charge and just let us do what we wanted. *They seek their own level*, Ada would tell people, and it was true. Mostly we sought each other. Still do.

The outer door opens: high-gloss older mother, lumpy toadstool son. She signs in at the window, he whips out a game and starts beeping away, *zzt, brrt, zzt*. The mother shrug-smiles at us, *boys will be boys*; I ignore her. Hilly smiles back, a smile that instantly dies as the receptionist calls "Hilly Polo?"

And I'm right behind her, because this is my plan: I'm going to sit in on the session, I'm going to observe, then tell them that this is Hilly's last visit. And when I get home, I'll tell Marshall and Ada, and that'll be the end of that.

But "Excuse me," the receptionist says to me, keeps on saying, more and more nervous until finally Molloy emerges, hands in his corduroy pockets, and "Sessions are for clients only," he says, frowning, looking from me to Hilly.

I'm looking at Hilly too, expecting her to say *It's OK, let him in*. But she doesn't, she doesn't say anything, just stands there gripping her backpack and looking at the floor.

"I'm her brother," I say.

"If you'd like to make a separate appointment—"

"See, that's the thing. We're not making any more appointments. Hilly's not coming here anymore."

He's not exactly happy about this, we go back and forth, louder and louder until "I'll call your parents," Molloy says, "*after our session.*" Hilly gives me a look over her shoulder, half-sorry, half-shrug; I slam the door for the receptionist's benefit, sit arms folded and pissed off until "I couldn't help overhearing," murmurs the high-gloss mother. Confidential lean, I can see down her blouse, pale chicken-skin cleavage. "We've had a few go-rounds with Dr. Molloy ourselves. He's fine for boys, you know, but I don't think he really resonates with girls."

"Yeah."

Hand in her bag, handing me a card, *Riverside Associates, Malcolm Roland, MD* and "He's marvelous," she says. "He put our Bree right back on track. It took forever to get her in, but he was completely worth the wait. If I could, I'd send him Jonathan"—zzt, brrt, zzt—"but his practice is limited to adolescent girls."

"Yeah?" I tuck the card away—limited to girls? what a sweet gig, imagine that waiting room—then catch sight of Game Boy shooting me this really hideous look, red cheeks and squinted eyes and "He's an *asshole,*" the kid hisses. "I hate Dr. Roland."

"Jonathan!"

"It's true! He's scary, he—"

"Jonathan, that's enough. —He's always had sibling issues," she says to me; the kid tries to say something else but "That's *enough,*" so I nod my thanks and pick up a magazine, leaf through it backward, an old habit. For a while Hilly and I used to write backward notes to each other; we got pretty good at it, too. Not just EREHT IH but real hieroglyphic stuff, no one could read it but us. We called it Otnarepse. (Think for a second, you'll get it.)

Finally the door opens again, Hilly with Molloy glowering over her shoulder and "Just get her records ready," I say, and lead Hilly out, she's been crying but not a lot and "So?" she says, as we get into the car. "What was that for?"

"So I found you a new shrink," I say.

She picks at her thumb, looks at me, stops. "I don't want a new shrink."

"He's 'marvelous.' Plus he only sees girls."

"So does a GYN. Ivan, I don't *need*—"

"Don't be stupid." It's just a lever, to pry her free from Molloy, she doesn't need this Roland guy either but since It took forever then in the meantime, while Marshall and Ada put Hilly's name on a list and feel they're doing something, I can get her back to her goddamn journal and all of this will fade away, sunset, bluebirds, happy ending and "What're you smiling about?" Hilly says as I peel out of the parking lot, cutting off a florist's truck and "Nothing," I say. "I just like helping people, that's all."

4

My journal is me, really. Ever since I could hold a pencil—I remember my very first one, a big fat yellow pencil, big drawing-pad pages with blue teddy bears on the front—it's what I wanted to do; all I wanted. While you were busy with your million things, whatever it was that year—fencing, jazz trumpet, comic-book art—I was tucked in the corner, in the car's backseat, writing. Because even then, my journals were always more than just something to do, they were where I lived my life. My real life.

My other writing—book reports, essays, Ada had me doing an essay a day for a long time, she picked out the topics ("My Chicago Vacation," "Freedom Is More Than a Word")—that was different, that was for school. And she used to enter me in all kinds of student-writing contests, Scholastic, New Voices, Homeschool Olympics; I won Best in District and Best in State two years in a row. But then I decided that competing against other writers was essentially bogus—I mean, what was the point? weren't we homeschooled because we didn't believe in tests and ratings?—so I stopped. Once in a while I'd write things for Ada, when she did her own why-we-homeschool arti-

cles, "Education and Learning" and all that: I'd stick in
some of my work, to help her make her points. But other
than that, and the research papers I sometimes still had to
do, I only wrote in my journal.

I wish I had another language—like Otnarepse, only
mine—that I could have used. I wish I'd let Marshall teach
me French—he was going to teach us both, remember?
But you didn't want to learn, so I said no, too. . . . Even
though the weather was getting warmer, an incremental
thawing day by day, it was still pretty cold out there at
night, sometimes my fingers got stiff, and you can't really
write too well with gloves on. Believe me, I tried. If I
hadn't been so worried that you were going to find out—

But there were compensations, too. The pure stillness,
like a lake without waves on a summer night. The feeling
of being more alive because everyone else was asleep. The
stars. The way a solitary car sounds, heading down the
street. A trundling possum, or the Oestermans' cat, Suki,
white and dainty and ferocious, drinking from their foun-
tain pond. The moonlight painting the long backyards,
the dark triangles of the fir trees, the charcoal-sketch lines
of the birches and the elms. The way the cold air felt going into my body, leaving warm again through my mouth.
Sometimes I'd lie down, my journal tucked safe into my
jeans, small square against the bow of my back, and let the
tarp settle against my face, like a dry plastic skin, a shroud.

But I didn't feel dead, I didn't want to be dead, not like
poor Elisha. I just wanted to be me. Even if that meant being sad. Or furious. Or alone.

Remember when Marshall had us into insects? The bee skep, and all those ant farms, and the cicadas, how they leave their old bodies behind. . . . That was why I'd started hanging out at Jarvis in the first place, why I'd made friends with Elisha and Kim, and joined Currents. Because all my life had been a chrysalis, with you, Ada and Marshall and our house; even though we did other things and saw other people, the summers at the lake, and all those homeschoolers' parties, it was still always just—us.

Now I was ready for something different. To climb out of my old body, and fly away.

But how could I explain all that to a psychiatrist? even if I wanted to? Dr. Rosen, at school, just gave me all these forms to fill out (*Have you ever used marijuana? Do you ever have angry thoughts?*). And Dr. Molloy—I didn't look down on Dr. Molloy the way you did, I knew he was only trying to help. Even though it wasn't working. The first thing he said when I sat down was *Make yourself at home.* I already had more than enough "home."

So I was happy that you got me out of there. They do pretty much what you tell them, Marshall and Ada, they always have; they trusted you to know what was best for me. Maybe it sounds ridiculous to say it like that, like they're bad parents, or weak people; we both know they're not. It's just that you were so right for so long.

5

THE FIRST THING I SEE IS THE JAKOBY PRINT, THOSE
brick-red and bruise-blue oblongs, no frame, hung there
on the wall like a floating thought. Very nice. Then the receptionist appears, white Hautbois jacket, it looks like,
sleek and severe and ultrapolite: "Miss Polo? Doctor will
see you shortly. Would you like some water, or tea?"

"No, thank you," says Hilly, turtling into her parka.

"Water for me," I say, checking through the magazines,
a very good selection: *Coliseum, The New Yorker, Green Light,*
which is what Hilly got from this guy, Dr. Roland, almost
right away; surprise surprise. Marshall and Ada were ec-
static, I was, let's say annoyed—definitely not part of the
plan, but what could I say? after I'd completely sold them
on this guy, pumping up the testimonial from the waiting
room mom—

*She said, solemn, he really resonates with girls. In fact, he
may—she said this, not me—he may have saved her daughter's life.*

*Really? Ada twisting her hands, looking from me to the
backyard window. She said that? Oh Marshall, we have to make
this work somehow, we have to get her in—*

—so here I am, making it work, adjusting circumstances to fit the script. My script. The Jakoby is a good sign, at least he's not some asshole with mountain pictures on the walls. . . . *He's an asshole. I hate Dr. Roland.* Well, that shows what kids know.

Now Hilly sighs and slumps down, chews her thumb that's gone past red to purple. With that thumb in her mouth and her raggedy parka she looks younger, like a kid herself. Baby sister, sad baby and "Don't worry," I murmur in her ear. "Already it's better than Molloy. And if it doesn't work out, I can get you out of this one, too—"

"You're the one who got me into it," as the door opens, the receptionist calls "Miss Polo—" and "Just a second," from behind her: a man's voice. Pewter gray Mitsubo suit, a hint of a tan. He puts out his hand, a vice president's grip, hard but not too hard and "You're Ivan Polo," says Dr. Roland. "Miss Polo's brother. Bob Molloy told me a bit about you."

I bet he did. "I just want the best for my sister."

"Understandable. Commendable." He turns on Hilly, still in the chair, and his smile mutes, becomes kinder: a kid-glove smile, like he's ready to handle something valuable, breakable. "Miss Polo, are you ready?"

Hilly looks at no one as she rises, angles past him, disappears down the hall and "I like the print," I say, nodding to the brick-and-bruise.

"It's not a print," says Dr. Roland, and shuts the door.

6

HE WORE THAT CHAIN-LINK BRACELET, REMEMBER?
I know you remember. Dull silver links like steel, but really expensive, you could tell; while he talked he played with it, it made a little sound, clink-clink. He sat watching me from a low-backed red chair. He had a tan.

Miss Polo, he said.

I put my hand to my mouth, put it back down. The blinds on the window made soft shadow bars on the walls. The room smelled like lemon, clean and cool.

Miss Polo, you're here for a reason. Do you want to tell me what it is?

It was so strange. When I looked at him, all I wanted to do was look away. Like backward magnets. Repulsion, it's called. I let the silence hang for a long time, until finally *My parents are worried*, I said.

Why is that?

Because my friend got sad and killed herself. Because they're afraid I might get sadder and kill myself. Because I spend a lot of time crying, or hiding in the backyard under a plastic tarp, writing a journal no one knows about. Stuff like that.

Ask them, I said.

There were two books on his desk, one called *Persephone's Crisis,* and some other thing about fairy tales. Once Ada had me rewrite a bunch of fairy tales for some contest. In my version, Little Red Riding Hood grew up and became the wolf. And Cinderella ran away from home in her glass slippers.

I've already spoken to your parents. What's your reason for being here?

I pictured you out in the waiting room, reading Coliseum, sipping your water; I couldn't wait to get back out there again. To be safe. . . . The smell of lemons. The bars on the walls. There were a lot of answers I could have given, but in the end the truth was easiest: *Because of my brother,* I said.

7

SEE, THERE ARE ALL KINDS OF CREATIVITY. HILLY'S IS the more traditional kind, do this and you get that: she writes down words, she gets a world. But I operate on a totally different premise. When I'm playing *Shards of Evil*, say, spray-gunning the demons and running up my score, or watching *Space Case*, or driving around in the city, trying to get lost, the whole time I'm *being Ivan*, I'm imposing my essential Ivan-ness on whatever situation I'm in, you follow me? I make up what's going to happen, adjusting for surface conditions, improvising, whatever; it's my art. Hilly has a bunch of notebooks. I have a life.

It's too bad it's not the kind of art other people can, you know, see. But that's the price I pay for being an original.

Like in jazz. Like Ornette Coleman, he plays kind of like I think; I'm playing him now as I stand smoking in the dark, watching Hilly in the midnight yard; she doesn't know I'm here; I think. You can never be totally sure with Hilly, which is why I call her Spooky; sometimes she is spooky. . . . It's not raining, but she's got the tarp up anyway, like she's trying to recreate our fort, or a safe house, a womb, whatever. Under there with a flashlight, like a kid reading under the blankets; is she reading? She's not writing, I know; I've been checking, but it's all still blank, untouched white. North Pole of the soul.

Today at dinner, Ada did some clumsy digging, so what did Hilly think of Dr. Roland? did she like him better than Dr. Molloy? while Marshall sat there in his Fastball Rehab sweatshirt, forking peas and trying to pretend he wasn't hanging on her every word, they both were, vibrating like quail dogs, but Hilly gave them squat, just eyes over the napkin, when she excused herself Marshall let out a whistling sigh and Ivan? Ada asked. What did you think? You liked the doctor, didn't you?

Sure. Especially when I found out that was a real Jakoby on the wall. Plus I got to spend twenty hot minutes with, what was her name? Keisha? in the waiting room, amazing tight shirt and no brains at all; we were on our way to the parking lot for a smoke and whatever when Hilly came back out, not crying, not much of anything really, just ready to go so See you next time, I told Keisha, and I'll drive her to her appointments, I told Marshall and Ada. I think she likes it better that way. And maybe I can even help out a little with her therapy, you know, talk to the doctor and stuff.

Because I wouldn't mind talking to Dr. Roland, I wouldn't mind at all. I looked him up online: college, residency, a million shrink boards, so far so boring. But: He writes books (Persephone's Crisis: Adolescence and Separation and After the Fairy Tale: Female Adolescents and Emotional Release)—OK, cowrites, there's another name before his on the cover, but still. And he collects art, Jakoby and a couple other top people. *And* he rubberboards. In Hawaii.

But the thing I liked best was something he wrote, a quote from one of the books: "I don't mind lying, but I hate inaccuracy." I mean, *yes*, exactly, I really couldn't have said it better myself so *Give it some time,* I told Marshall and Ada, and went out for a cigarette, blowing smoke now at the white blades of the ceiling fan as outside the tarp ruffles and settles, a shed plastic skin, Hilly emerging? or just settling in? To do what? Maybe I should just go and snatch it off, see what's going on under there—

—as a parkaed arm pops out, waves once, slides back in: she knows I'm watching.

Spooky, huh?

8

SOMETIMES WRITING IN MY JOURNAL TOLD ME things that I didn't know I knew. It has to do with tapping into the unconscious, what you used to call deep-sea fishing. Like I'd start writing a list—of places I wanted to go someday, maybe, or books I wanted to read (Paris, Seattle, Iceland; *Durina's Dream*, which Elisha gave me, *The Haunting of Hill House*)—and as I wrote it, the list would start to mutate into something else: a happy memory, a forgotten joke, a map to what might be. *A sea-change / Into something rich and strange.*

So one Wednesday night—midnight quiet, lying on my stomach under the tarp; Marshall and Ada were sleeping, you weren't home—when I started making a list about Dr. Roland—

> *window blinds like bars*
> *bracelet*
> *what color eyes?*
> *read me like I'm a book*
> *Persephone*

—I paid attention. I didn't like going to his office, being there with him, but I wasn't exactly sure why, besides the obvious. If I could have, I'd've talked it over with you, the way I always did, always used to, checking my impressions against yours, seeing if you saw what I saw. Because there was something about Dr. Roland I wasn't sure of, something totally different from Dr. Molloy and Dr. Rosen, something hard and calm and

dirty

but not sexy-dirty, not like that at all. There are plenty of older guys who go hunting for girls that way. Like that one dad we used to see at fencing, remember? The one you called Mr. Lolita, who always sat with the sisters, or the really young moms. Guys like that look for the weak girls, the ones they can bully and flatter into doing what they want; anything they want. But Dr. Roland wasn't like that, he was more like—like—

the cave

As soon as I wrote that, the pen went dead in my hand. I lay there, heart pounding, open-eyed and listening, like Suki the cat listens for a mouse. Or the mouse listens for Suki.

The faint rustle of the tarp, like insects' wings. The smell of damp soil. Ada's snowdrops, white like sleeping moths in the darkness.

I didn't write any more that night. I almost tore that page out, to throw it away, but instead I folded it carefully back onto itself, so I couldn't open onto it by mistake. The cave.

What would have happened, if I had talked to you then? Would you have listened? Like Elisha on the roof, staring into the darkness. Would anything have changed?

9

SUN'S SLANT THROUGH THE WINDSHIELD, TRAFFIC'S crawl past a stranded sideways semi, three Wednesdays in a row now and she still hasn't said one word about any of it to me, not one, a bad sign so "Hey," I say; I turn down XRZ. "So what's the verdict?"

She's picking the end of one draid; she doesn't look up. "On what."

"On your guy. Dr. Roland."

"He's not my guy." Her voice is dry, her eyes are too, even though she was locked in the bathroom before we left; I heard Ada talking to her through the door, wheedling, that come-on-good-puppy tone that drives Hilly crazy; crazier? I mean I kind of expected this crying stuff to be over by now, that girl's been dead for what, three months? so "You know," I say, cutting into the left-hand lane, "it's one thing to, like, grieve. She was your friend, OK, whatever. But when it gets obsessive—"

"Did he tell you that? What did he say to you?" All eyes now, her laser stare, in fencing it's called "presentation," where you offer your blade to the opponent and "Calm down," I say, deliberately looking away; that's called "absence of blade." "He just asked me for my take on things—"

—just like that, just as she was coming out: *Could you step in for a minute?* so I did, past Hilly's startled frown, past the iceberg receptionist, down the hall into his office: blood-red chairs, light gray walls, gray-and-white watercolor and *Is that a Jakoby, too?* I asked, just a guess, but he looked pleased.

You've got quite an eye, he said. *Are you an artist yourself?*

Yeah, I said, because if it wasn't true exactly the way he meant it, it still wasn't inaccurate. *I am.*

I believe in art. I believe it has a lot to teach us. He might be Marshall's age, or maybe just a little younger, but they couldn't be more different: this guy is so obviously on top of things, totally in charge. But relaxed, too, playing with his chain-link bracelet, little clinking sound as *For example,* he said. *I've learned a lot from your sister's writing.*

You read Hilly's stuff? She gave it to you?

No. Clink-clink. *Your parents shared some of her work. They thought it might help me understand her. And it does. . . . You're very close to Hilly. She listens to you.*

Yeah. Pilot to copilot. She does.

Leaning forward in the chair: *Did you know that she wants to discontinue her therapy?*

Already? But I'm not ready to stop coming here, to this office with its art and its girls, last week I met Johanna, blond hair down to here, boobs to infinity. . . . *How's it* going to hurt Hilly to spend a few extra weeks sitting in a chair while someone talks to her? Answer: It's not. It can't. So *She needs to keep coming*, I said.

Your parents—they respect your judgment? As regards your sister?

I got her here in the first place, didn't I?

He smiled then, I smiled too and I think *we're on the same page, Ivan—do you mind if I call you Ivan?*

Not at all. Malcolm.

And then he really smiled, shook my hand, led me back to the waiting room, to Hilly's stare, watchful, wrathful, the same stare she's giving me now, sideways on the seat, plucking at her Medusa hair and "What things?" then before I can answer "It doesn't matter," she says. "I'm quitting therapy, I'm telling Marshall and Ada today."

"No you're not."

Startled. "Yes I am. What do you mean? *Yes, I—*"

"Hilly, come on. It can't hurt, just to sit in some guy's office—"

"Is that what you told him? Or what he told you?"

"Look," as we make the loop onto Oak, too fast, I hate it when she argues with me. When she won't agree. "You sleep in the backyard, you cry all the time, you don't write anymore. So a reasonable person might say that you have a problem, a *reasonable* person might—"

"Ivan, don't. Don't do this—"

"I'm not 'doing' anything, Spooky."

"Don't call me that!" as I screech into the driveway, just

missing Marshall's blue Saab; she yanks her parka hood back into place, is she crying? No. Definitely not. Out of the car, past the house to the yard: tarp time? Definitely yes.

Jesus! Why won't she just listen to me?

10

THE GUIDE WARNED US, I REMEMBER THAT: PANIC can kill you. *No matter what happens, stop first and think.* Gathered all together before we went inside, passing out big red waterproof flashlights—and you were clowning, tipping my helmet over my eyes, tossing pebbles at me as *Pay attention*, the guide said sharply, said it twice. *You need to know this stuff.* But you didn't listen.

How old were we then? six and eight? on one of our experience vacations, Ada's choice this time: caving. Lava tube, limestone, Plato's cave, Lascaux; a cavers' group is called a grotto, I remember that, too. And the way the sun touched the edge of the ridge, a white line, pure dazzle: I stared at it as long as I could stand, then shut my eyes quick to see the mirror image, the blazing red negative light.

At first the cave was so beautiful, even better than all the pictures Ada had showed us. And a totally different kind of darkness, like weight, like something you could hold in your hand. The sound of water, trickling. Cave crickets. You were right up front, answering all the questions you possibly could, getting on the guide's nerves. I was way in the back, trailing behind the other family group, a mom and dad and two daughters. One of them had a Disney T-shirt. The other kept giggling, giggling at everything. I remember thinking she was a little weird.

And then I was gone.

Just like that. Down the rabbit hole, just like Alice. I don't know where the flashlight went. By the time I screamed, was able to scream, everyone was already off searching another passage; you told them I went that way. You weren't lying, you were just—wrong. But you were wrong so seldom, even then, that Marshall and Ada believed you.

Have you ever been all alone in the dark? I had a light on my helmet, we all did, but when you're alone the light looks different. When you're all the light you have.

Panic can kill you.

When I closed my eyes, I was the negative.

I don't remember how they finally found me. They thought I had a broken ankle—later the doctor said it was just sprained—and the guide was totally furious. I grabbed onto his neck like I was drowning, and I wouldn't let go, not even for you.

Goddamn kid, the guide said, but he didn't mean me.

11

"IVAN? CAN YOU HELP ME A MINUTE?"

Ada in the backyard, frayed blue gloves and rusting shovel, trying—unsuccessfully—to dig up a browned-out shrub. She gardens a lot, or used to. Now all she seems to do is think about Hilly, worry about Hilly, and talk about Hilly endlessly on the phone. She even calls Grandma Kitty, her mother; she can't stand Grandma Kitty. I suppose it's because Marshall won't talk to her anymore, at least about the situation: *We found Hilly a very good doctor, she's in treatment, what else can we do?* I heard them arguing last night, after their blowout with Hilly. Their fights are always the same: Marshall repeats himself a thousand times, and Ada cries.

Now I push against the shovel, push harder, and the roots come free: ugly, blackened, wet; rotten. The space in the ground looks like the socket of a pulled tooth. Ada lugs the shrub up and onto the wheelbarrow, *thump.*

"Thank you, honey. . . . Ivan—"

Oh here it comes: *Can I talk to you for a minute?*

"—can I talk to you for a minute?"

"About Hilly."

"Yes." Glancing toward the house, Hilly's window. "You know, your sister's very angry with us."

"I know."

Angry's not the word. Hilly said no more therapy, fini, but they told her they'd committed to twelve sessions from the start, that it was the only way Malcolm was willing to take her on. They also told her, because she'd already guessed and was screeching, that yes, they'd showed Malcolm her writing. Just a couple of old essays, he already gave them back, but Hilly's acting like he pried open her head and pissed on her brain.

"Dr. Roland was very impressed with her work," says Ada, with a kind of sad pride. "It was why he made room for her in his schedule." A pause. "Ivan, you like Dr. Roland, don't you?"

"I already told you I did. Why do you keep asking me?"

She pokes at the shrub's black roots. "Because your sister—because she doesn't like him. At all."

Mm-hmm, I got that. She doesn't like me much either these days, she hasn't talked to me since our— disagreement in the car. Which is really shitty of her, she knows I can't stand the fucking silent treatment. . . . She can't tarp out because Ada's here in the yard, but as soon as she can, she will. Hiding under a plastic sheet, and she thinks I'm delusional?

"Hilly doesn't like anything now," I tell Ada, and take off for a drive.

I've always loved riding in cars, planes, trains, whatever: it's like being in two places at one time, two states, static and active. Plus driving makes certain things easier. Getting away from the house when I need to, buying cigarettes, meeting girls. . . . People think if you're home-schooled, you're isolated from the outside world, like you sit around in your pajamas with an abacus or something. Really it's just the opposite: you're not stuck in some kid jail all day, you're free to go where you want to go, teach yourself whatever you want to learn; to *experience*. Especially if your parents trust you. Or if they can't stop you. Same thing.

One of the things I learned was that lots of high school girls skip school and hang out in the park; they like to meet guys with cars. Even some college-age girls. Once, Marshall asked me if I was still a virgin. Like it's any of his business.

I'm not in love, I told him. *I know some girls, but—I'm not in love.*

I'm glad to hear that, he said, all father-and-son, and patting my arm. Ada knows better, I don't know how but she does. Motherly radar, or something. She gave me a box of condoms and told me to make sure and use them. Hilly saw the box and laughed her head off: *Ada gave you those? Doesn't she want grandchildren?*

Later she wrote about it in her journal: *Ivan's getting*

sticky with some girl! wonder who? "Getting sticky." Where'd she get that from, her cheerleader friends?

When's the last time I heard her laugh?

She's a pain in the ass now, but still, nothing's really changed between us. It can't. Pilot to copilot, everything is under control.

12

THE NEXT WEDNESDAY DR. ROLAND GAVE ME HIS book, *Persephone's Crisis: Adolescence and Separation*, the cover a picture of a girl on top of a mountain, her hair blowing in the breeze, dark clouds massing over her shoulder.

It's only fair, he said. I read your work, I'd like you to read mine.

The blinds were half drawn, letting in slices of sunlight, catching silver fire on his wrist. I didn't say anything. Since I couldn't talk things over with you, I talked to myself, and that was what I had finally decided: to just sit there and wait it out. Marshall and Ada could force me to go to the appointments; they could show Dr. Roland my writing—how could they? Even if they thought it was to help me. Would you cut out my heart, I said, to save my life? But they didn't understand. . . . Even though it was just those old school papers, not my real writing, my journal. They would never have done anything like that to you.

But if they could make me go there, they still couldn't force me to talk, to do anything other than look at my hands, look at the blinds, look anywhere but at Dr.

Roland, still talking about his book, all the research he'd done, all the interviews with teenage girls, girls just like me and *I'd be very interested in your critique,* he said. *I think we reveal a great deal of ourselves through our work.*

I looked down at my hands again, at my red-and-purple thumb. You'd yelled at me again in the car: *Stop chewing your goddamned fingers!* You thought it was worse than it was, like my thumb was infected; you didn't know the purple was from my journal ink. . . . I could almost feel you, out there in the waiting room sweet-talking that bimbo, the one with the big breasts, to go out to the parking lot with you, to get sticky. The girls were part of the reason you wanted me to go there, why you kept telling Marshall and Ada they were doing the right thing.

Girls have always said yes to you, haven't they? even though you never seem to treat them very well. Is that why you never had a girlfriend? a real, relationship-type girlfriend? Why you always met them in parks and clubs, saw them once or twice and then dropped them?

Or maybe you were trying to flirt with the receptionist, *Merry Ceretski* on the little gold nameplate, even though she was older and way out of your league. Always perfectly dressed, perfect makeup, everything, she looked like a model, but always unhappy. Or mad.

Dr. Roland was talking again, no matter how I tried to drown it out I still heard every word. *You're familiar with the Persephone myth?* in this oh-so-kindly way, like he knew he was smarter than me, knew all sorts of things that I didn't, but was being very careful not to rub it in, because he was my doctor. Which of course rubbed it in. Which was what he meant to do all along. *Proserpine is another of her names—* I know, I said.

Then you know that it's often seen as a negative story, but I think—and I said so in that book—that it represents a very positive time in a young woman's life— Getting kidnapped to hell. Sure. Very positive.

—a time of transformation. Leaving home, leaving your parents' control, making your own way and on and on, all about girls and their families, me and my family; was I angry at my family for making me come here? Was I expressing my anger by not expressing it? because that was a very common defense, especially among young women. Or was I expressing my anger through my writing? The samples he'd seen ("samples," like they were something he was deciding whether or not to buy), while very fine technically, were unrevealing personally. *But You keep a daily journal, isn't that right? You know, I'm writing another book, about young people and creativity, and I'd like very much to include some of your work. Is that something you might be interested in? Being published?*

Persephone ate six pomegranate seeds, and because of that she had to stay in hell half the year, every year. Forever. For six little seeds. You have to be so careful what you swallow.

Who's Drew Bishop? I asked. It was the other name on the book cover, Drew Bishop and Malcolm Roland, M.D.

He didn't say anything for a second, then, brisk, *He was my assistant.*

Then why is his name first?

Silence. The sun. More silence. Finally *Your brother,* he said. *He's not very much like you, is he?*

I remember being scared, then. Usually everyone said, *You two could be twins! two peas in a pod!* But he saw, he knew, that we were different. And the way he said it, like he'd done some careful thinking about you. Like you . . . amused him.

He's an interesting boy. His real name isn't Ivan, though, is it? It's Jeffrey.

When I heard that, I felt sick. I know you hate the name "Jeffrey," you always have, you always said "Jeffrey Polo" could be anybody, some stupid bullethead jock, stupid dead uncle, when I'm old enough I'm changing it legally. But how did Dr. Roland find out? You didn't tell him, I knew that, you never tell anyone. Did Marshall and Ada tell? Or was it on some medical form or something?

Why does he go by "Ivan"? Does he think—

Leave him alone, I said. My voice sounded small; I tried to make it strong. *His name is none of your business. He's none of your business.*

You're very close to Ivan. He listens to you.

I said, *leave him alone.*

The chime went off then, a muted sound; it meant the session was over, and I could go, escape, but as I got up from the chair *I'd like to see your journal,* Dr. Roland said. He actually smiled. *Give it some thought. Serious thought.*

Go to hell, I said, without knowing I was going to say it, and then I was gone, out of the chair, the room, I heard him stand up behind me so I made my steps long, I wanted *out*—

—and I almost crashed right into Merry, there by the waiting room door and *Sorry,* I said. My voice sounded funny, shaky. *I didn't see you.*

She put her hand on my arm. She had narrow gray eyes, cool and still. Did you ever look at her eyes? *Are you all right, Miss Polo? Would you like some water?*

No, I just—I'm going, and I did, into the waiting room where you were, sitting there thinking how smart Dr. Roland was, with his books and his art and his cool magazines, his giggling girl patients. I know you love it when people are smart.

And *Ivan?* from behind me, right behind me, *Could you step in for a minute?* and before I could say a word, you did; the door closed on you, swallowed you, as the bimbo looked at me and said *So who is that guy?*

That guy. My brother. Pilot to copilot. You want so much to be better than everyone; you need it. Top of the fencing tournaments, the trickiest pieces in the trumpet recital, the most kills logged in *Shards of Evil.* You've always been that way. Remember when we used to make those little books together? Sheets of construction paper folded and stapled, you'd write a page and then I'd write a page, drawing crayon pictures, pushing the story along. Then I started getting good at it, as good as you were. You never wrote any stories with me after that.

The way Dr. Roland said it: *He's not very much like you, is he?*

In the cave, it was your voice I heard most clearly, calling for me. When they finally pulled me out, you cried.

He's my brother, I said to the girl.

He's hot, the girl said. *But kinda weird. . . . Is he really, like, a scientist or something? He said he was a social scientist.*

You came out grinning. You had the Persephone book in your hand.

Here, you said to me. *Take your medicine.*

13

PERSEPHONE'S CRISIS IS, PARADOXICALLY, ALSO HER great opportunity. She goes into the darkness to meet her destiny. She is on a great adventure, the ways girls and young women are also on a great adventure, into the marvelous unknown of maturity. Her parents cannot make the journey for her. Like Ceres, their job is to wait until she comes back, reemerging whole on the other side of the darkness.

Which makes me, what, Hermes? Do you know the Persephone myth? She's hanging out in the fields with her maidens, tra-la, until the king of the underworld spots her, and takes her downstairs for a hot time. Next thing you know, her earth-goddess mother, Ceres, is flipping out and cursing the earth into permanent winter, because she can't find her baby girl. But then Hermes proposes that they travel to the underworld to bring her back: Hermes, the patron of thieves and tricksters, of people who live by their wits. Completely my kind of guy.

But lo and behold, poor dumb Persephone has already eaten of the fruit of the underworld, six red pomegranate seeds (sounds like an anorexic to me). So she has to spend half the year down there, which is why we have winter.

And when she comes forth to visit her mommy, Ceres is so happy that she makes it spring and summer. . . . As a seasons myth it's OK, but I like it much better the way Malcolm's using it, as a coming-of-age story. Because sometimes you just have to go to hell to grow up.

Which is why I've got no sympathy for Hilly—for this current tantrum, or hissy fit, or whatever you want to call it. Malcolm's not killing her, for christ's sake, he just wants to help her get some perspective on her situation. Like I tried to do. But she'd rather hide under her tarp and pout. She's turning into a fucking mushroom out there.

The mistake many parents and teachers make with girls and young women is to deny their active participation in the maturation process, to try to "protect" them from the next step in their lives. The darkness is absolutely necessary. There is no gain without risk.

See? Isn't that cool? No gain without risk. And the risk is no risk at all, really. What's so risky about sitting in a chair? And what's-her-name, Johanna, she's been going there for six months already, and she thinks Malcolm's a perfectly good doctor. She also thinks he's kind of hot, for *an older guy. Plus did you know he drives a Jag?* Johanna thinks I'm hot, too. I think Johanna's already had breast implants, but hey, I'm all for self-improvement.

What a girl or young woman needs most on this voyage into the darkness of self-discovery is a reliable guide. Not someone to lead her, for she must uncover her path for herself, with all of its pitfalls and wonders—

"Pitfalls and wonders." I like that, too.

—but a guide who can help her explicate each phase of the jour-

ney, recognize the signifiers, and empower her along the way. This is where a gifted therapist can be invaluable.

Not to mention a clear-eyed, hardheaded older brother who refuses to take her histrionic shit, who's willing to act for her own good, whether she sees it or not. A smart brother, and a smart therapist, who sees just how helpful that brother can be. . . . We had a nice little talk the other day, Malcolm and I.

14

OUT ON THE BACK PATIO, NEW SUNGLASSES, FEET up, and smoking, you were reading Dr. Roland's book, or pretending to. You hate sitting outside, so I knew why you were really there: to spy on me.

I had my sunglasses, too, those nerdy ones Marshall used to wear; you couldn't see my eyes. I hadn't slept all night, out in the dark yard, writing and writing, my hand aching with cramps. Now I stood, arms crossed, over you, trying to sound stern.

Give me that, I said. *It's mine.*

Don't be such a bitch. You blew smoke in the air, a wavering stream. *I'll give it to you when I'm done, I read faster than you do.*

Which was true. And I didn't want to read that awful book anyway, I just wanted to get it away from you. . . . I'd started writing about Persephone in my journal. My own Persephone. An alternate fairy tale, like I used to do for Ada—

—who was watching us from the kitchen window, the way she always did, that anxious smothery way, like a mother bird wishing she could stuff the babies back into the eggs. The night before, before I went outside, I'd gone to her, there in the family room flipping through *Backyard Landscapes*, her teacup sitting untouched on the end table. Alone, because Marshall had gone straight from work to a community center meeting, arguing over how many times a year people could put out their grass clippings, or whack their weeds, or something. She always used to go with him to those kinds of things. Then she stopped going and stayed home. She was almost always home those days. Thinking, or worrying, or talking on the phone.

So I sat on the edge of the sofa, in the lamplight half circle, next to her. And I got right to the point, the way you always did, looking her straight in the eyes, holding her with my stare.

You said I only have to go to twelve sessions, right? So this week makes four. Eight more times, right?

Oh honey, taking my hand; hers was ice cold. She looked so incredibly tired. *Try not to concentrate on anything but getting better. Try not to—*

Eight more times. Right?

That loving, giving-in sigh. The background music of our lives. *Yes. OK. Eight more times.*

So *It doesn't matter anyway,* I told you on the patio, trying to provoke you, make you mad enough to forget about the book, to toss it down. *I won't be seeing Dr. Roland for very long. Just eight more sessions, that's it.*

Says who?

Says Ada. Last night I talked to her, and she—

And you smiled, that sunny smile I hate the most, the

one you used to have when you flushed my Barbies' heads down the toilet, watching them bob and spin, sucked down to jam up the pipes and *That'll be up to me and Malcolm,* you said.

What're you talking about?

Didn't he tell you? You took off your sunglasses, tossed them on the grass. *I'm working with him now. On his book.*

I remember exactly how I felt then: like that carnival ride where the floor drops out from under you, and all you can do is hang on to the wall. "Working with him"? What could that mean, oh my God, and *You can't,* I said, which was absolutely the wrong thing to say, never say "can't" to you, but I was—stunned, I guess, it was so much worse than I'd imagined and *I'll tell,* I said, stupid, like a two-year-old. *I'll tell Marshall and Ada*—

And you laughed; you had me and you knew it and you laughed. *I'll tell them myself,* you said. *They'll love it. Especially Marshall, he's always after me to "do" something, make something of myself. . . . Anyway, what's not to like? I'll be cowriting a major shrink book, I'll meet his editor, I'll be*—*You know, Hilly, if you weren't so jealous, you'd be happy for me. Here Malcolm's giving me this great opportunity*—

He's not giving you anything, he's—Ivan, *he's bad, OK? He's bad and he doesn't*—

Bad? You laughed again, the way you laughed at other people, but sharper, meaner, because it was me. Like when you used to pull off your mask at the end of a fencing tournament, and laugh at whoever you'd just beaten, pretending to be a gracious winner: *Nice work, dude. You al-most had me. Almost.* Remember when that kid tried to stab you with his épée? *He's not "bad," stupid. He's the smartest per-son I've ever met in my life.*

And I stood there thinking, Should I tell him? what Dr. Roland, "Malcolm," is really doing, should I tell? even if it hurts him? so *He asked me first,* I said. I slid my sunglasses off, *so you could see my eyes. He wanted to use my journal, to publish it, but I said no.*

Bullshit.

Ask him.

You're a liar, Hilly, which you know I'm not, we both know you're the one who lies: to get out of things, to get what you want, you always have. But you were mad then, horribly mad, you slammed the book shut and *Fucking jeal-ous,* you said, you yelled, *fucking jealous liar* as you stormed off across the yard, kicked the plastic watering can so hard it flew, tumbling gush and spray of the water inside, till it hit a bush and cracked some branches. Then I heard the car, your car, snarl in the driveway, squeal down the street—

—and then Ada was out of the house, eyes wide, want-ing to know what had happened; but how could I tell her? How would it help? so *It's OK,* I said. My hands were trembling, so I stuck them in my armpits. *We just—had a fight.*

About what?

The broken bush, black wood cracked white, like a

bone; the water oozing into the ground. You'd left your cigarettes on the deck chair, your sunglasses on the grass, which would make you even madder. . . . Where did you go, that day? I never knew. But I can guess.

Nothing, I said.

15

A LONG TIME AGO, WHEN WE WERE LITTLE, WE
went caving, Hilly and me. Flashlights and too-big mining
helmets, the damp basement-smelling air, the idiot guide
droning on and on; he was a real asshole, I remember
that. Pompous and incredibly rude: *Give someone else a chance
to talk, kid.* Big fucking know-it-all, except he didn't know
it all, did he? When it mattered?

I remember I told Hilly there were bat families living
on the ceiling, generations of them, bat grandmothers and
grandfathers, roosting up too high to see; I told her all the
crickets in the cave were blind. Maybe they were. There
are such things, anyway.

She was dawdling behind us, and then she wasn't. I
told them she'd turned off to the left, the twisty branching
cavelet the guide wouldn't let us explore. I remember the
older girl in the other family group, a fat girl in a red
Mickey Mouse shirt, tugging at Marshall's arm, saying she
heard someone crying under our feet.

I remember when they pulled Hilly out, like Persephone, from underground; her ankle was broken, except
it wasn't. Her eyes were huge, she hung on to the guide's

shirt like a baby monkey. A freshly tortured baby lab monkey.

I was going to tell them eventually. I only said what I said because of the guide.

Did I mention he was a real asshole?

16

L ET HIM GO, I SAID.

Sitting there in his sleek gray suit, legs crossed, in the red chair, not behind his desk, like we were equals or something. He didn't pretend not to know what I meant.

I'm not forcing your brother to do anything, he's more than happy to contribute. And I need a writer, Hilly, a young writer to provide the counterpoint for my book: Voices from the Future. *It's about gifted young people, and the way they process their world through art.*

His clinking bracelet; the afternoon light. Lemon scent. What did it smell like in hell? Like brimstone, or burning sweat? Or nothing? Persephone would know. Persephone had the experience.

Ideally, we'd have used your journal, it was what I'd intended from the start. But since you weren't interested—you made that very clear—I approached your brother.

So it was my fault, then. I thought you only, you just—did girls. How can your book be written by a—

It will be "written," sharply, by me.

Then why do you need—

If you're not interested, Hilly, why do you keep asking questions?

I remember looking down at my hands, seeing that I was picking at my thumb without knowing it, picking and peeling the skin there. The red wink of blood, the exact same shade as his chairs. I'd been up all night, thinking about your saying *I'm working with him now*. About what that might mean. Could mean. Would mean, if someone didn't stop it.

It wasn't a carnival ride, it was a torture device, you strap yourself in with your eyes closed because you know it's going to hurt, hurt like hell but OK, I said. My voice sounded like I couldn't breathe. *I'll do it. But you have to let my brother go.*

Are you serious?

Yes. Take me instead.

He didn't say anything, he just smiled, a modest smile, gracious winner, no one would ever try to stab him. Until it was too late. *Well, I'm very glad you've reconsidered, Hilly. Very glad. Why don't we start with your journal? You bring me what you've got, and I'll see.*

There's another hell myth, about Orpheus. He went down to rescue his wife who died, what was her name? Penelope? No, Eurydice. He sang with his harp for the god of the underworld, who let Eurydice go on one condition: that Orpheus lead her out, but not look back. Ada never asked me to rewrite that one.

All right, I said. Next week I'll bring something.

He leaned back, relaxed in the chair, happy. If someone like him could be happy. *Tell me, did you read my book?*

Ivan's got it.

Take a look at it. I think you'll be interested. You more than Ivan.

Seven more sessions. I had to be so careful, I couldn't write just anything for him, he *was* smart, very very smart. But so am I. And I was scared. So I had to be even smarter.

Panic can kill you, the cave guide had said.

17

THE GIRL'S NAME IS LISA, OR LILA, OR SOMETHING like that, I forget, and who really cares anyway. It's not like we're plighting our troth or anything, here in my car's backseat, her blond hair swinging back and forth, back and forth, my fingers digging hard into her thighs. Finally we disentangle, she lights one of my cigarettes and "What dorm're you in?" Rubbing sweat off her face with her shirt; very classy. "Staley, you said?"

"Uh-huh. Staley."

"Then do you know Jake Caruso? He's in my econ seminar, he plays lacrosse, well he used to but then he got suspended, and—" on and on and on, unless you stick something in her mouth it's just one endless sentence. So while she drones, I light my own smoke, and think: What am I going to show Malcolm tomorrow? I wrote some stuff, nothing I really loved, but there was this one riff on sibling rivalry that I liked. It wasn't, you know, anything totally earth-shattering, but I thought it was pretty good, and pretty important, too, to point out that gifted kids grow at different rates; grow emotionally, I mean. Like Hilly. We may be only two years apart, but she, she's an

emotional infant. An emotional *retard*. You wouldn't believe what she did to get even with me. Bit off her head to
spite my face.

"—drinking these shots of Black & Blue, I didn't like
pass out but I got really drunk, and Jake—"

But Malcolm is cool about the whole thing; he's very
flexible. And it'll be good for Hilly in the end, he thinks,
very therapeutic. . . . See, I'm not mad at her, I'm not vin-
dictive. Even though she basically stabbed me in the back,
went sneaking to him to cut me out of the process. Malcolm explained it to me: it's not that he wanted her journal *per se*, not for the book, our book. But of course he
wants her to write. Like I've been saying all along, if she
was writing in her journal none of this shit would have
happened in the first place.

"—asked Jake if he knew me. But then *she* said—"

We even laughed about it a little, Malcolm and I.
I mentioned that I'd told Hilly the good news about the
book—and I had to smile, I couldn't help it: it's not as
easy as it used to be to smash one across the net on her,
and the look on her face proved that I did it, she looked
absolutely *stunned* and *She may be jealous of you*, Malcolm said
to me, leaning back behind the desk, clink-clink. That's a
Tiffany ID bracelet, by the way; he told me. *It's nothing to be
angry about, or even surprised. It would be natural, don't you think?*

I—well, yeah. Naturally. But you know, *Hilly's really smart too.
Her IQ is—*

*It's not about intelligence, Ivan. It's about experience. Your experi-
ence of the world is so much wider than hers.*

Which could not be more true. I mean, look at me right now, in this twilight park, with Lisa or Lila, who's a sophomore in college, she said; and look at my future, my name on the cover of a book, *Ivan Polo* in streamlined sans serif, my picture in the back—

"—because I *don't*, right? I mean I never even saw the guy before! But Jake got like all pissed off—"

—which of course is why Hilly's doing the sabotage thing. It is only natural, really. If shitty. But she'll get there one day herself, she'll be published too, I know it. Even when we used to write those stupid little staple-books together, I knew that she was really— But I outgrew that kind of stuff long before she did, I had too many other things to do.

Anyway it's all OK, her silent treatment–punishment, her bogus attempt to compete, everything. And eventually she'll catch on, catch up. Pilot to copilot, nothing's really changed, it's not like we're—

"—listening? You're not even paying attention to me!" Lisa/Lila's pink-lipped scowl, arms crossed over her bare white breasts, they *are* pretty spectacular breasts so "Sure I am, babe," as I toss my cigarette out the window, and reach for her again. "I heard every word you said."

18

THE TARP HAD A NEW CRACK, ANOTHER SLIT WHERE water sifted in, a late-night misty rain. Something rustled softly past in the grass: Suki, hunting? Or a little possum, or a vole, maybe. I shifted on the lawn-chair cushion. My legs were cold and numb.

Things are different underground.

That's how I started it, the dupe journal, how it started itself.

Underground, geography doesn't matter. There are no vistas, no landmarks, no horizon. There is only up. Or down.

The walls sweat magma, volcano blood. Small things shriek and skitter past, brushing her ankles, scratching her skin. One path looks like another, and every path is dark. Persephone has no guide, or map. She uses the map in her own head, she writes it as she goes along. Every day she takes another step.

At first I thought I couldn't do it after all. I lay there on the grass, breathing in and out, thinking, How can I lie, when my journal is me? But I had to write something, have pages, enough to seem plausible, like it was something I was working on every day.

So then I thought I'd try to simulate my real journal, and write about things that were true: how I missed Elisha, and Kim, and Currents, and the afternoons hanging out at Jarvis. How I used to kind of like doing my projects for Ada, her essay ideas like a puzzle I had to solve; and how she'd pretty much stopped asking me to do any schoolwork at all now, as if I were too "sick" to be required to do anything, too mentally frayed. Like my cracking-up tarp, the cheap plastic splitting at the seams.

But I couldn't make that work, you could tell, he could tell that it was fake. You can't write a lie about the truth and make it any good.

And then all this came out instead, this Persephone story, one page and then another. In a dreary way I was even proud of it; it was pretty good writing.

Persephone learns that the dark is a kind of cocoon. Some creatures grow strong there, outside the light. Other creatures die.

In the land of the dead, only one thing matters: getting out alive.

Sometimes it seemed like we were living in a kind of hell, too. Ada was getting more and more upset, constantly talking about me and my "problems," to her friends who were tired of hearing it, to Grandma Kitty, who never got tired, who always had something new and awful to say. Grandma Kitty even talked to me once, her voice soft and slippery in my ear, asking me all kinds of questions about Ada, like wasn't this all her fault somehow? Wasn't it all because she was too permissive, too softhearted, too much of a marshmallow to put her foot down? Things would be very different around there, Grandma Kitty said, if I were in charge. I bet they would.

And Marshall was spending more and more time out of the house, working even more hours, going to all kinds of meetings, running away from Ada. And from me. And from you too, because you were so awful then—I'm sorry, but you were. So incredibly arrogant, so totally full of yourself.

But that's not right, is it? You weren't full of yourself, you were full of Dr. Roland, of "Malcolm." You were being Malcolm, like a little kid dressing up for a play, for Halloween. Dressing up to be a monster. . . . Was he somehow sticking to you, clinging to you, like napalm, burning, you can't scrape it off without scraping off your own skin? Or was he more like an infection, silent inside your head, in your blood, crossing all your boundaries, seeping like sewage to where you can't reach?

Watching you in those days was very hard. So Marshall ran away. And Ada cried.

I didn't cry. Hunched up out there in the blue-tarp light, sun on its surface like underwater, my head on my knees because I missed you, the real Ivan. My Ivan. Even though I'd sacrificed myself for nothing, even though Dr. Roland was taking you anyway, even though you wanted to go. . . . I should have known better, I thought. I should never have trusted Dr. Roland to turn you loose.

But I had, and I'd lost, so maybe—I thought this sometimes—maybe I should just concentrate on saving myself, on getting out of the darkness alive. Because no one was coming to save me, no one was bringing ropes and light and a guide who knew how to squeeze through rock; there was no you, even, waiting for me to come up out of the hole. This time I was all alone.

But I just kept thinking, what if all this—the way you mimicked Dr. Roland, his way of talking, of pausing between words, his taste in art and books, his way of thinking—what if it somehow became permanent? if you got sucked so far in you could never get out? Like napalm turning into skin. Like your face becoming his. . . . I kept seeing you in my mind's eye, in that office, your legs crossed in the red chair, and Dr. Roland just sitting there, smiling, nodding, waiting. . . . I just couldn't leave you. Even if you hated me. Even if you didn't care.

So I kept on writing.

Persephone hunts down food in the dark caverns. She is hungry, so hungry, but there isn't much to eat, nothing like the world she left behind, the world of Ceres, of growing things and rain and plowed earth. Her mother feeds the whole world. But down here there is no light, and nothing ripens, it only swells, bloats outward like a boil. So she becomes a skillful hunter, with the few tools that she can find. She has no choice.

Skillful, maybe; I hoped so. But careful, yes. So careful. When Wednesday came again I got myself ready, I let myself feel the anger, the white-hot furnace of it, blast furnace, carried it like a shield and You fucking lied to me, I said, as soon as I sat down. My voice was shaking; I let it. You said you would let him go.

He just shook his head, with resignation, with mild regret; he wasn't even smiling. It was like talking to a picture on the wall. *I'm afraid that's not possible anymore. Ivan insists on being involved.*

So what? Aren't you the one in charge? For a second I thought that might work, that kind of challenge, but *Your parents,* he said, *are perfectly comfortable with my seeing you both,* which was maybe true and if it wasn't you could make it true, they'd take your word before mine, they always had. I wouldn't have been in that office otherwise. *Ivan's a client now. Just like you.*

He shouldn't be here. You're the one who—

Your brother, he said, *feels that you're trying to compete with him. He feels this very strongly.* This time I knew he was telling the truth. Maybe telling the truth was like lying, for him. *I believe it would do more harm than good at this stage, to discourage Ivan. I believe he can still be helpful. You and he are very much attached, I know, you and he are almost like—*

Don't, I said, staring past him out the window, the spring afternoon like another country, sweet and very far away. All the tulips were out now, swaying on their long stalks; the dead grass had all come back, new and green. I *won't talk about me and Ivan with you.*

Quiet, then. He started looking at the pages I'd brought, fourteen pages, folded in half to make them look thicker. Black ink on white notebook paper, the copy was easy to read, even in my bad handwriting, even though Dr. Roland wasn't too happy with a copy, he wanted to see the real thing but *Forget it,* I said, *I'm not bringing you my original.*

He didn't push it. He was being accommodating, the way you are when you're winning.

That's all right, Hilly. As long as you're writing.

Quiet. The whisper of the paper. I heard the phone ring up front, where Merry sat. Today she was wearing a green-and-gold high-collared jacket, and a long gold chain, with a little green carving dangling at the end. She had smiled at me when I came in, a small twitch of a smile; no smile at all for you, sitting there jingling your keys, clink-clink. I wished for the millionth time that I'd gotten my license; I could have driven myself, you would never even have seen Dr. Roland. . . . We hadn't spoken at all on the drive over; we hadn't really spoken for weeks. Forever.

I missed you so much.

It wasn't just that you were mad at me, you've been mad at me a zillion times before, every time I did something you didn't like. But this was totally different, this was like you were gone, you were . . . A hundred times a day I wanted to go to you, talk to you, try to get you to see what was going on, what I was trying to do. But whenever you looked at me you seemed to look completely through me, as if I didn't even exist, or didn't anyway to you. You've done that kind of stuff before to Marshall and Ada, but never to me. And it felt horrible.

Did Dr. Roland tell you to do it? No. This was you.

The pages unfolded, and rustled; Dr. Roland was smiling. Even looking past him, away from him, I saw it, the curling edge of that smile.

I see you're using the Persephone myth. That's very *intriguing.*

I didn't answer.

Why did you choose—

Your book, I said, which was true but not the way he thought it was; you wouldn't even let me have the stupid book, let alone read it. Not that I would have. I didn't want any more of Dr. Roland in my head. But let him think I was "inspired," or something, by his wonderful work—because he did, you could tell, sitting there in the chair clinking his creepy ID bracelet. That cheered me up a little bit. It isn't easy to fool smart people. But sometimes they fool themselves.

I'd like to set a goal for you. Say, twenty pages a week. And we'll discuss them.

Twenty times five more sessions is one hundred. One hundred pages, that's most of a book right there, isn't it? Wasn't he planning on writing any of it himself?

I don't want to "discuss" anything. I'll write them, and that's all I'll do.

There wasn't much he could say to that, and I wouldn't talk anymore, so he let me go early, out before the chime sounded, to see Merry in the hallway, green and gold, carrying some files: *Oh, Miss Polo. Session finished already?*

Yeah.

*Your brother just stepped out. With Miss—*and she made a motion over her own breasts, big-balloon motion; I smiled and so did she, that narrow smile. *Would you like some water while you wait for him? Or tea?*

No, thank you.

She was always nice, to me at least if not to you. How could she stand being there, day after day? Like working in a sewer, shoveling toxic waste and *Do you like working here?* I asked, without knowing I was going to. *You like Dr. Roland?*

Her look changed then, focused and sharpened, as if I'd been rude, worse than rude, as if I'd been obscene and *I'm sorry, I said right away, I didn't mean—*

This is my job, she said. Two lines appeared on her forehead, hard lines carved right between her eyes. *Everyone has to have a job.*

I'm sorry, I just—

You're very young, Miss Polo. You don't have to support yourself yet, you— But *you'll learn. Everyone does. I did.*

Experience, I said.

Exactly, she said, relenting. She was smiling again, but it wasn't her real smile. *Experience makes all the difference in the world.*

19

I'VE FUCKING HAD IT WITH HILLY.

I know how that sounds, believe me. I know how it feels. But she's turned into such a, such a *liability*, that I can't even deal with her anymore, I can't justify expending the energy. And you have to wonder, how much of this is from the situation, and how much is pure latent bitchery that was going to come out sooner or later, no matter what happened. The first time she's really seriously thwarted, you know, out gushes all this . . . bile.

The competition business, fine, I can handle that, more than handle it. Even her stupid silent treatment—because she was starting to crack, I could tell. I can read her like Otnarepse, I know what goes on in her head. She'd sidle up beside the computer when I was working on the book, or watch me sideways in the car, you know, when she thought I didn't see. It was so obvious that she wanted to get close to me, but as soon as I'd look up—trying to make the opportunity, you know, the space for her—she'd run away. Leave the room, or turn her head, or scuttle out to the backyard, to her psychotic little plastic world.

See, what really hurts—I mean it doesn't hurt, you

know, I'm not mortally wounded or anything. But I *am* really pissed, in a way I never thought I could be with Hilly. Because I did everything I could think of, everything right. Who stuck with her through all her weirdness, when she had to go rushing off to Jarvis, those brainless girls and their brainless magazine? Who held her hand when she cried over dead what's-her-name, Elisha? Who got her away from Molloy? Who got her in with Malcolm? which means got her writing again, which is what I wanted, what I fought for, all along.

And then she doesn't even tell me. She doesn't even let me *read* it. That is so fucking low.

Malcolm says it's excellent stuff, which is no surprise; I knew it would be. There's really no reason for him to keep pointing it out to me—

"Hilly's so talented, isn't she? And she writes so simply, she doesn't need any verbal pyrotechnics, any camouflage. She's the real thing."

—especially when he won't show me the goddamned pages. I asked, even though I shouldn't have to, I have a better right to see them than he does. Than anyone. And there's no need for him to get all patient-confidentiality with me, technically I'm a "patient," a client, too; it's family therapy now. He said we needed to do it that way for him to justify setting aside the hour to meet with me, like for his insurance company or something.

And anyway, he's already told me plenty about Hilly's sessions, asked for my input and advice, because she's definitely not getting any "better," even if she is writing again. If she wasn't so stubborn—like with her tarp, for God's sake, even the neighbors are asking questions now, Mr. Oesterman cornering Ada in the driveway: *Gee, what's Hilly up to in the yard? I see her out there all the time, digging under that plastic sheet.* I told Ada to tell him, number one, it isn't any of his damn business, and number two, Hilly's doing a science project. The effect of rot on living matter. That ought to shut his ass up.

But nothing's really wrong with Hilly. I wrote some about that, in the new pages I gave Malcolm.

Sickness can be a mask the person dons, to conceal her insecurities or her latent fears. Freud discusses this at length, as does Jung. Sickness can also be utilized as a mode of defense, a deep moat of illness around the castle of personality. Or sickness can be a desperate attempt of the personality to flee from unpleasant or painful facts it does not want to confront.

Which I thought was pretty damned good, especially throwing Freud and Jung in there, I figured his editor would appreciate that. I ask if he's read my pages yet, I mean he's had them for two weeks, but he doesn't answer, just asks more questions about Hilly, does she seem to be eating all right? does she need sleeping aids? which means drugs although "She'd never take them," I say, shaking my head, blowing smoke out the window; sometimes he lets me smoke in his office. "I mean never. She won't take an aspirin. She doesn't even like to drink coffee—"

"Can you think of anything else that might be helpful?" *Clink-clink.* Another Mitsubo suit today, matte black, very sharp. I could see myself in a suit like that, only no tie, because I don't do ties. Maybe a *Shards of Evil* T-shirt underneath, that would look cool.

"Well, she needs to give up the silent treatment, for one thing, that stuff just doesn't work on me. And she could climb out from underneath her stupid tarp for a—"

"She's still using the tarp? You're allowing that?"

Me? allowing it? and "Hey, I don't—" but he's staring at me, and I'm not sure what it is I don't, what I wanted to say, I mean if he's so worried about the tarp why didn't he bring it up before? He's the doctor—

—but he's still looking at me, eyebrows up, and "I'd think very closely about that," he says. "Very closely."

"You mean—what do you mean? Take it away from her?"

He shrugs. "There are ways to help it happen," and then lets it hang, lets me figure out the rest for myself—and really, now that I think about it, he's right, it's the right thing to do. Why *do* I allow her to squat in the yard under a piece of plastic, like a, a garden gnome or something? How could that possibly make her anything but worse?

See? I care about Hilly. I never stopped. She's the one who changed. Like in the car today, on the way back, that dumb deli commercial, *light lunchtime fare with downtown flair*, but when I sing it in my lounge-lizard mode she gives me this *look*, like I'm a moron or something, Easter Island everlasting and "Oh go to hell, Hilly," I say, louder than I meant to. I mean I wasn't that mad, it just—slipped out.

And she looks at me with her big Spooky eyes, her hand goes to her lips so "Get your thumb out of your mouth," I say. "You look like a two-year-old, I'm ashamed to be seen with you."

But she doesn't take her hand away, she just—looks at me. And finally I have to look away, or crash into a light pole or a truck or something, I have to drive the car because she's too lazy to get her driver's license, does she ever think about that? Too lazy to drive, or work at her therapy, or try to get better, she doesn't even deserve to be in a fucking book, let alone write one; I don't feel sorry for her at all. Not at all.

So talented, the real thing: right. And what does she do with it? Hides under a piece of plastic. True genius.

I punch the radio louder, XRZ, make the turn onto Oak, light up another cigarette—I've smoked almost a whole pack already today—but as I pull up into the driveway I see Hilly twist in her seat, bending in on herself, crying, not the way she cried for what's-her-name, Elisha, but silently, hopelessly—

—like some other time

—when?

And the memory surfaces, all at once, from so long ago: the little dead thing in the waves. We were out at the beach cottage, the one in my wallet picture, but older, seven and five probably. I was building a sand fort, I wouldn't let her help so she'd wandered off, gathering shells or stones or something with her little blue shovel and pail. Then all of a sudden she came running back;

she'd found some little animal, a mouse or something, floating in the surf. Tearing over at top speed, wet hair flying, to me, there on my knees in the damp sand, she wanted me to wake it up. That's what she said: *Help* him! *Wake* him up!

So I tried. I petted it, and blew air in its face, I turned it upside down to get the water out, but it was no use, we both saw it was dead, too dead to be helped, and so I carried it in my pail back up the beach, back behind the cottage, and we used our shovels to dig a little grave.

And she cried then, squatting by the sand pile . . . just the way she's crying now, slow and heartbroken and hopeless, crying for what won't change and "Spooky," I say, and put out my hand, uncurl hers from the fist it's in. "Oh, Spooky, come on. It'll be OK. It's all going to be OK."

"Please," she says. She can barely speak; I can barely hear her. "Please, Ivan, don't go back, *please* don't go back there anymore."

"Jesus," I say, but not mad. "How screwed up are you? There isn't anything wrong with my being there. And Malcolm isn't 'bad,' he wants to help you. He got you writing again, didn't he?"

"I didn't do it for him," she says. "I did it for you."

I don't say anything for a second. Then "Let me see it," I say. "Let me read it first, like I used to."

She doesn't speak, she just looks at me, wet gaze locked on mine. Then "Only if you don't go back there," she says, throat full. "If you promise me. A real promise."

"Oh, Hilly, come on, don't do this to me. I know you're jealous about the book, I don't blame you, but you can't just expect me to—"

"Oh, God, why can't you see? I don't *want* to be in his book, I don't want *you* to be in his book—"

"It's not 'his book,' it's a collaboration between him and—"

"He's not collaborating with you, Ivan, he doesn't even want you! He's just using you to get at me!"

She stares at me, and I stare at her. We're a foot apart. We're a million miles apart.

"Spooky," I say. My voice is flat. "That is just so fucked up."

"Ivan, you have to listen to me, I love—"

"Fuck you."

"Ivan—"

"Fuck you," and I'm out of the car, cigarette smoke in my eye, right eye burning, weeping, I slam the door so hard the whole car rocks on its springs, my feet make dark marks in the backyard grass.

Using you to get at me. Like I don't matter—me, Ivan—at all.

That's it, Hilly. You're done.

20

You THREW MY TARP AWAY. RIPPED IT TO BLUE rags, then stuffed the strips in the trash, hanging out so I could see them. I wasn't mad, not really; I knew it wasn't your idea. It was Dr. Roland again, divide and conquer, he'd been doing it all along. And it works, if you let it.

I wish I hadn't said what I said to you. I should have known better—I did know better. That's not the way to make you listen. And you were hurt, I knew it; I hurt you.

And it was already too late.

You got what you wanted, some part of my mind said, a cool dry voice. *Independence, right? No more family chrysalis, no more Ivan. Congratulations.*

This is not what I wanted! I cried back, but the voice was silent.

Almost sunset, the last of the day's light, lighter later every day. Our seasons change the way they should, things sprout and grow and bloom, so many flowers: the spill of violets through the grass, sweet purple and white; the lilacs' scent a cloud in the air, a beautiful, invisible gift. The pale blue clematis climbing on the toolshed, we got Ada that last Mother's Day, almost a year ago, forever. You picked it out, remember? Everything alive and growing, except me, dreary on the patio, churning out the week's twenty pages. Why did I even keep on? What good could it do anymore?

Deep-sea diving. Caving. Going under.

Now when I wrote in my other journal, my real one, Persephone was somehow in there, too, everything tangled up, bleeding together; why? Double journals, another kind of backward writing. *Linking hands with Persephone, we are the same, the same age even. Did she have a best friend, a sister, a brother? Who did she cry for, who did she leave behind on the surface, when she was dragged down to hell by the king of the darkness? That's worse than this, isn't it? Is it? Or are all the hells the same, is every darkness just one darkness after all?*

And what does the light look like, when you finally come up for air?

If you come up.

Darkness, the feeling of panic, of floating, imploding. A cave leads to the underworld, that's how Orpheus went down. And Persephone. Everybody going to hell, digging up bones, breathing in the sulfur smell; no, that's the Christian hell, isn't it? Greco-Roman hell has a river, and a three-headed dog. . . . I never understood how anyone could think it would be hot in hell. Heat is alive. So hell would have to be cold, terribly cold. Absolute zero.

Hey, kiddo. What's up?

Marshall was standing over me, smiling; he looked so tired. He had drinks for both of us, mocha cappuccino from Shiner's, his favorite. He lowered himself in slow motion into the wrought-iron chair, as if his back was bothering him; it always goes out when he's stressed. You'd think he'd use some of those therapy machines at the clinic, but no. *You writing?*

Uh-huh. I closed my notebook.

Something for Mom? Or for you?

For me. I knew what he wanted to talk about, what he came out for so It's OK, I said, looking straight at him. *It was time to get rid of it. The tarp, I mean. I'm not mad.*

He made a sigh, a smile. *Oh I'm glad you feel that way, kiddo. Really glad. Your mom and I—we thought that you might be—*

I know, I said, then drank some mocha, so I wouldn't have to talk. It was much too sweet, like liquid candy. Thanks, I said.

My pleasure. It's nice to know I can still give my girl a treat.

Inside we could see Ada, framed in the window as she talked and paced, neck and shoulder hunched to keep the phone in place. She was talking to Grandma Kitty, she never paced like that with anyone else, like an animal in a too-small cage, a prisoner. . . . You weren't home, you'd gone out, no one knew where.

And as if he'd guessed my thinking, heard your name in my head *Your brother,* Marshall said. *He's really upset.*

I know. I can't help that.

Can I? with his eyebrows up, like if only he tried long enough, worked hard enough, he really could. Somehow this broke my heart, that hope, that innocence but *No, Dad,* I said, as gently as I could. *This is between Ivan and me.*

I know that. It's always been between Ivan and you. He sighed again, small and dry, and in that sigh I heard years of, what? frustration? or maybe a kind of longing, the way you feel when you're always on the outside looking in. When you know you always will be. *We do our best for you and Ivan, we try our best. We always have. If there was another way, a better way, we didn't know it.*

I know. It's OK.

We just tried to do our best for you. For both of you.

Dad, you don't have to—

No, *it's all right. But it's*—it's not easy to know exactly what to do sometimes, what to think. A pause. *You two aren't the easiest kids to raise, you know. Especially your brother.* He smiled. So did I. He looked down at the table, his hands on the table, then up again at me. *Hilly, is Dr. Roland*—

Good lord, from Ada, letting the door slam behind her. *I thought I would never get off the phone.* Standing over us, as if we were a campfire, rubbing her arms like she was cold. She always looked haggard after she talked to Grandma Kitty, Marshall saw it too and *What news from the dragon lady?* he said, trying to be funny; it wasn't funny, no one laughed. Ada took a sip of his mocha, made a face.

There must be a pound of sugar in here, she said.

Ada? I said, half turning in my chair. *Next Wednesday, could you drive me?*

She and Marshall looked at each other. I knew what they were thinking, they thought I didn't want to ride with you. But that was OK. *Sure, honey,* Ada said, and reached to squeeze my shoulder. *I'd be glad to.*

Really I should be driving myself, I said. My fake-interested voice, like I cared what I was saying. *I need to get my license.*

Yes you do, Marshall said, as if he was relieved to talk about something normal for a change, something with no doctors or sadness or Grandma Kitty in it. *Why don't we call, what was the name, Roads Scholars? The place Ivan went to? The guy seemed like a pretty good instructor, we could maybe get you into the fall session—*

And so we talked about nothing, driving schools, funny learner's permit mishaps on the roads, until it got too dark to see one another, out there on the patio. Then we went inside, we went to bed, I went to bed because there was no reason to be outside at night anymore, was there? And it didn't matter that the tarp was gone, I could write my real journal anywhere now, sitting cross-legged in the middle of the kitchen table if I felt like it, you wouldn't look at it. At me. You wouldn't come near me anymore. . . . I missed you so much, like a part of my heart that never stopped hurting. Like Elisha, only worse, because you were alive. Alive and there, but gone.

I lay on my bed for a long time, looking at the ceiling, the moving moonlit branches, a collage of shadow and light. I used to love this room. My desk, an old-fashioned pigeonhole writing desk; my faded-denim quilt; my souvenir shelf, piled with shells from the lake, postcards from the Smithsonian and the Metropolitan Museum, old brochures with curling edges from all the experience-trips we'd ever taken. On the closet door were the faded traces of your painting, that blue-and-white cartoon face, from my monsters-in-the-closet period. SAFE, you had painted in pink above the face, and IN HERE in green below. Safe in here.

It was after one when I fell asleep. You still weren't home.

When Wednesday came, of course you were furious, and since you weren't speaking to me poor Ada had to take the brunt—

God damn it! I can drive her, I've been driving her all along! Why do you always give in to her? Doesn't anyone in this family have any BRAINS?

—but I stood right beside her, I kept the keys tight in my hand, until finally I got her in the car, into the waiting room, me staring at the wall, her trying to read some dumb design magazine until *Miss Polo*, Merry called, then leaned out and smiled at Ada, her cool neutral smile. *This is Mrs. Polo? Very nice to meet you.*

You brought your mom today, Dr. Roland said, as soon as I walked in, but I wasn't going to talk about Ada, or why you hadn't come with me; you're so smart, Doctor, you figure it out. Instead I handed him the week's installment, the Perils of Persephone, I hadn't even read it back through, just copied and stapled—

There are only eighteen pages here.

That's all I had time for.

We agreed on twenty.

That's all I had time for.

—and sat there staring at my hands while he read them, listening to my breath going in and out, thinking

Will this even work, will she even talk to me? Will she tell Dr. Roland what I say? But still I had to try, I had to find out.

So as soon as the chime went so did I, rushing back to the waiting room where Johanna sat, Chanel baseball cap, top two buttons of her shirt undone, examining her teeth in a glossy red purse mirror, she had her lips skinned back like a horse's and *Can I talk to you for a second?* I said. *Out in the hall?*

She squinted at me, as if I were far away, or someone she'd never seen before. Maybe she really didn't recognize me. And already Merry was at the door—

—but instead of calling Johanna, she called to Ada: *Mrs. Polo? Doctor would like to speak to you for a moment.*

And my heart jumped, a panic surge, oh my God now what? but Ada was already up, purse nervous in her hand, too late to stop her so I turned back to Johanna. Hurry, hurry, use the chance—

—but before I could say a word *You're Ivan's sister*, she said, as if she'd solved a problem. *So where's Ivan? Didn't he come today?*

No. Listen, I have to talk to you, about Dr. Roland. I have to ask—

Well is he going to come later? Like to pick you up, or—?

No. I came with my mom. Listen: how long have you been here?

She checked out her teeth again. *I don't know. I left at like four-twenty or something, what time is it now? . . . You don't have any floss with you, do you?*

I mean as a client. How long—

I've got some fucking popcorn or something stuck in my tooth, and it hurts. She rotated the mirror, tilted her head, and I closed my eyes; I must have been desperate to think I could talk to her, conspire with her, that she could even remotely help; help me do what? Stage a big walkout, fracture his practice? The rise of the teenage girls. . . . In my mind's eye I saw Elisha shaking her head at me, half annoyed and half amused, saying *Droll. Very droll, Hills.* Elisha would have helped me, with her hair-trigger bullshit detector, her laugh like a bright clean breeze. Elisha and Kim. Kim had transferred out of Jarvis right after Elisha died. Her old e-mail didn't work anymore, I had no idea how to get in touch with her.

Listen, Johanna said. She leaned close to me. *Has your brother got a girlfriend or anything?*

And then Ada was coming back out, smiling a little, the dazed, tentative smile you wear when the news is bad, but not as bad as you thought it might be. And Dr. Roland was right behind her, one hand on her shoulder. Smiling at me.

I had never hated anyone before, and I didn't hate him then, but I felt . . . something. Like a sound, a humming buzz in my head. White noise. Absolute zero.

I'm glad you came in, he said to Ada.

Thank you so much, Doctor, Ada said. She was still gripping her purse. *We appreciate everything you've done for Hilly.*

I didn't say anything, there or in the car, I just sat with my head against the window. I knew something was coming, something I didn't want to hear and *Honey?* finally Ada said.

My eyes closed. Red glow, negative light. *What?*

I know we agreed, but—what would you think of another twelve sessions? Or even six? Dr. Roland thinks you've made some real progress, but if he had more time with you—

I felt the road through the glass, vibration, speed, and I thought: She can never come near him again, she's like a flag in the wind, a twig in the ocean. . . . That hand on her shoulder. That chummy, silver-bracelet hand.

No, I said.

Honey, please, just think about—

No! which made her flinch, just a little, the way she sometimes did with you. She'd never done it with me before. Poor Ada. Poor all of us.

I hadn't *seen* Elisha, and she died, stepping barefoot into thin air. You couldn't see me. Dr. Roland thought he saw me in the pages he read. What did I see when I looked at him?

That smile. And something else. What?

If there's hell, then there's heaven.

Elisha, I thought. *Help me.*

21

THE OFFICE BUILDING LOOKS TOTALLY DIFFERENT at night. No foot traffic on the first floor, no office staff, FedEx, coffee-kiosk girl. Just a cleaning crew with their battleship-gray supply cart, muted vacuum growl. And a different security guard, an older white guy with aviator glasses and a sloping beer gut. As soon as he sees me, he motions me over.

"I'm here to see Malcolm Roland," I say. "He's expecting me."

The guard takes his time checking me out: deliberate look at the book in my hand, at me again, like he's pretty sure I don't belong here. Before, this would have completely pissed me off, but now I know better. Like Malcolm says, act on the situation, don't let the situation act on you. Finally the guard nods—"OK. Go on up."—like he'd like to stop me, but can't think of a good-enough reason.

He can't stop me.

The dry purr of the elevator. The dermatologist's office is dark, the medical records suite is dark. Riverside Associates has its waiting room lamps on, twin golden glow, empty furniture like a stage set. Merry the unmerry receptionist is gone. The door is unlocked.

Malcolm is at his desk, reading; he doesn't look up, just nods as I walk in and sit down. The silver desk lamp, like an insect's curved antenna, throws a circle of white on the magazine in front of him. The Jakoby painting really seems to be floating now, gray and white in the air, in the dark.

"Did you bring it?"

Her journal looks like a toy on the black desk: smudged white pages, purple ink. He takes it, opens it, leans back. The light keeps shining on the magazine, on a half-page photograph of Malcolm standing at a podium, shaking hands with some bearded guy. I read the headline upside down: "Healing Words Reap Professional Benefits."

She should have known better. She knows me.

Malcolm glances up. His face is in darkness. "She'll miss this."

"I don't care if she misses it."

"I mean, she'll know it's gone."

"I don't care about that either."

He smiles. He closes the journal and smiles. "You've been amazingly helpful, Ivan. I'm very pleased." He leans forward again, and the desk light hits his bracelet, makes a sharp silver flash.

"You got that at Tiffany, right? Do they still—"

"It came from Tiffany," he corrects me. "I got it as a gift, from my mentor. A graduation gift." He smiles again;

this one isn't for me, it's for the past, for his mentor, whoever that is. Malcolm is my mentor now, I guess.

"She thinks you're bad," I say.

He puts the journal in his desk drawer, clicks it shut, a
tiny final sound and "It always seems uncomfortable," he
says, "to go past what you thought were your limits. But
limits are just an illusion of the thinking mind. You've
learned that already, obviously. Hilly will learn it someday,
too. Intelligent people usually do."

"It's not about intelligence, it's about experience." I
read that somewhere. Or maybe I made it up. "And what's
'bad,' anyway, I mean who's to decide? Something that
seems wrong to one person might turn out to be completely right."

"As you say, experience will show you the difference."

Experience. What you are times what you want equals
what happens to you. What you make happen. I've always
made things happen, but now I'm operating on a whole
different level, being Ivan to the tenth power; the hun-
dredth. And when the book comes out—

"Did you send that outline to your editor yet? The, the
part with my stuff?"

"Not yet."

"You said last time that you were ready to send it, you
said you—"

Malcolm looks at his watch. "Don't worry. And thank
you again, Ivan."

Outside, the moon is shining, big full moon, white

wash across the cleaning crew's big green van, my car, and Malcolm's. What's-her-name, Johanna, is wrong, it's not a Jag, it's a black Mercedes with vanity plates, GOODDR. I'd prefer a Jag, myself, but in the end a vehicle is just that, a construct for taking you where you want to go. Like my writing is doing for me. Like I'm doing for me.

Some people would say taking her journal was wrong, but those terms are just more constructs, you know? Right and wrong. There's only action. And reaction. Like physics. I act, Hilly reacts. Then I act again.

We'll see who wants who, won't we?

Back in the car now, my foot on the gas, it's ten-thirty and I'm off to meet Lisa and a few of her girlfriends, we're going clubbing tonight. Lisa still thinks I go to State, but so what? Let her think what she wants. Let all of them think whatever the hell they want.

22

THE CURRENTS ROOM LOOKED EXACTLY THE SAME. The scuffed layout table, the chairs and computers and sticky Coke cans, the hang gliders on the yellowing REACH UP HIGH! poster, with Elisha's scribbles in the bottom corner, where she always tested her pens. Red—green—darker green. Black.

I had my old purple pen in my backpack, and a fresh new untouched journal. My old one, the real one, was gone. As soon as I missed it, I knew what had happened.

You let him into my head.

Oh, Ivan. I knew you could get mad, really mad, and weak, scary-weak. But my *journal?*

Now I knew for sure I was alone.

Footsteps then, coming down the hallway, a brisk voice, *Hello, who's in here?* It was Mrs. Price; as soon as she saw me she smiled. *Hilly! Well! How are you?*

I made a smile back. *Oh, I'm fine.* Lie number one.

Well, I'm very glad to hear it. And to see you. Mrs. Price had gotten a new haircut, very short, she'd dyed her silver hair blond. Red button earrings, an oversized Jarvis sweatshirt. *We've really missed you around here.*

From the window by the fire exit door you could see into the courtyard, bright with flowering bushes, red and white, the Jarvis colors. I used to sit there with Elisha sometimes, while she had a quick cigarette. No one was out there now.

Want to see the new issue? as Mrs. Price clicked it up on-screen, the familiar logo, the boat in the sunrise tide. Currents. Riptide. Undertow. You can live through an undertow, if you don't fight it; that's what Kim had told us. Her younger brother Martin was a long-distance swimmer, he'd gotten caught in an undertow once. *You don't fight it,* Kim said, *you use it.*

The masthead was different, of course. No more editor Elisha, no more Kim. No more me, either. Some of the names I knew, but at least a third I didn't. The mix of writing seemed to be pretty much the same, some fiction, maybe a dozen poems—

—vampire poems, tales of true TV romance, your smirk, but you were mad about it, too, weren't you? Mad that I wanted to do it, to go somewhere without you. Mad that I could.

Mrs. Price clicked through the rest of the pages, the layout still incomplete. *We're going to put the memorial page here*—for Elisha, you know, *a tribute page.* She raised her eyebrows a little. *You did get my letter? Asking for a submission?*

No. Did you take that, too? No, I didn't.

Oh. I mailed it quite a while— *Well, anyway. There's still some time. You'll write something for us, won't you?*

Sure, although I didn't know if I could write about Elisha for other people to read—though Dr. Roland already had, hadn't he? Stuff no one was meant to see, no one but me, oh God damn him—

—as the door banged open, a girl I didn't know, blue jacket, wild corkscrew black hair and Mrs. P, loud, *Mr. Anderson says no way we can*—and then she saw me, and stopped.

Gina, this is Hilly. Hilly used to work on Currents. *Hilly, Gina is our interim editor, she'll be taking over for good next year.*

Gina made a half-smile, not especially friendly. I didn't know her, she'd never worked on Currents before. A freshman, maybe? She had a tattoo or a stick-on or something, a dark blue star beside her left eye.

You knew Elisha? she asked, like a challenge.

Yeah. We were friends. We spent hours here, in this room, at this computer. Where nothing is now but memory. *Do you know Kim Fischer? She*—

No.

You're always welcome to come back, Mrs. Price said to me. *We can surely use you, right, Gina?* The blue-star girl frowned and left. Mrs. Price smiled at me, took some papers from the table, a battered red folder and *Actually,* she said, *I'd always hoped you'd transfer here, Hilly. You still could, you know. Junior year. . . . Think about it, won't you?*

I knew I never would, with Elisha and Kim gone, never come back to this room again but *I will,* I said, *I'll think about it.* Lie number two, was I turning into a liar? No, oh please no, so I opened my mouth to say something, to take it back, but Mrs. Price was already leaving, leaving me with the computer, the Coke cans, the faded pen scribbles, no one there, not Elisha, not Kim, not even me; why did I think there would be? Because I needed someone so terribly? Because I didn't know what to do?

Elisha, I thought, if you're not here, where are you?

Silence. The room. The boat in the sunrise tide.

Slowly, moving like I was made of lead, I reached to click on the screen saver, picked up my backpack, stepped back into the hallway where *Wait!* called blue-star Gina, her arms full of magazines. *Hold the door! —Where'd Mrs. P. go?*

I don't know. Do you need some help with those, or—?

No. She clumped past me and dumped them on the table, fat spill of beat-up fashion magazines, *Glamour, Vogue, Pink Lady,* and *Thanks,* she said, the way you say it when you want someone to leave, but I didn't, I just stood there looking at her, until finally she looked at me. And *Don't worry,* I said, just the way Elisha used to say it, when people were panicking on deadline, or the computer ate their reviews, or whatever.

I'm not worried, Gina said, but then she laughed, a stiff little bark, like we both knew she was lying. *What I am is going fucking nuts! This is a nuthouse, you know it?*

You'll be fine.

And then I left, quiet down the quiet hallway, out to the warm afternoon, the long oaky avenue in front of Jarvis where two boys drove slowly by, yellow truck with

blue-tinted windows, beeping at some soccer girls on the
practice field. One of the girls yelled something back, and
all the girls laughed. The normal world. It seemed so . . .
sweet.

You'll be fine. Why did I say that? How did I know it?
Actually, Elisha would probably have liked that girl.

When I got home, I didn't go inside, just sat waiting
by the driveway, on the green edge of the grass, the black
shadow-line of shade, my head on my knees, until you
pulled up: way too fast, radio too loud, you almost didn't
see me, you had to really jam on the brakes—

Jesus Christ, I could have hit you! You looked scared. Did
you think I was trying to kill myself? *What're you sitting
there for?*

It's time to go.

—to the car, to the office, a couple of times you
glanced over at me, did you think I was going to bring it
up? or yell, accuse you, denounce you? What good would
that have done, for you or for me? So I didn't. I didn't
even look at you.

And I didn't look at him, either, there in the red chair,
waiting for me to say something, too, waiting for me to
scream or cry or tear the room apart. . . . Where is it, I
thought, is it somewhere in here or did he take it home?
Did he read all of it already? Did he read it all the first day?

Imagine a monster seeing you naked. Imagine how
that would feel.

Do you have some more pages to give me, Hilly?
No.

Imagine the monster, smiling at you.

Is there anything you'd like to talk about today?

No.

When I came out—early, very early, Johanna wasn't even there yet—immediately you tossed down your magazine and went in. Merry looked at you as you passed, a measuring look; did you notice? I don't think so. Then she stepped into the waiting room, and closed the door behind her, a careful click.

Miss Polo, she said softly. *I heard about your diary.*

Her voice, the dry kindness of it, made me instantly want to cry, cry the way I hadn't yet, all the tears held down inside. Instead I forced it all back again.

Thanks, I said. My brother—

I know about your brother, she said. *Your brother did a terrible thing.* She was close to me now, leaning down, her gold-and-green pendant dangling near enough to touch: I saw it was an elephant, a little carved-jade elephant. *Listen. Doctor needs your diary, you understand?*

What do you mean?

She glanced back over her shoulder. She had tiny wrinkles around her eyes, her mouth: frown lines. Strain lines. The elephant swung back and forth, captive on its chain. *For the book,* she said. *His book. But you're a minor, he can't use your work without your parents' consent. You know that, don't you? They have to sign and say it's OK.*

My parents will do what my brother says.

She didn't answer that, just looked at me. Then *You're a very strong girl, Miss Polo. I saw that right from the start.*

Why is he doing this? I said. I could feel the tears in my throat, I could hear them. *Why me?*

He always needs someone, she said. *He can't do it alone. Can't, you understand? He has to have someone to . . . feed him.*

The phone started ringing, two rings, three. She bent so close her hair touched my cheek, like Elisha's had.

Give him nothing, she murmured, and hurried to answer the phone.

23

I T TAKES ME FOR-FUCKING-EVER TO GET IN TO SEE him—without Hilly, I mean. Merry the bitch receptionist is all arctic on the phone, even worse than normal, like she's got some secret grudge against me or something: No Doctor can't fit me in on Friday, no he can't see me on Monday, and maybe not Wednesday either, Doctor is very very busy. . . . I mean, come on. No one's *that* busy. In fact, if I didn't know better, et cetera et cetera, which totally can't be true but still is the first thing I say when I finally do get in, early Monday morning, way-too-early morning when I should definitely still be in bed: "So Malcolm. Didn't you want to meet with me, or what?"

He's in shirtsleeves, no tie or jacket, he's got a stack of files and paperwork, a sharp little matte black laptop; he doesn't look up as I sit down. "Time is very tight for me right now. Why did you want to come in?"

Why? Why the hell do you think? "The *book*," I say. I have more pages to give him, fourteen pages; I worked like mad to finish them, polish them, I must have read over them a hundred times. And I think I made my points pretty well: point number one, that an organism needs to grow, no matter if that growth causes pain, like roots breaking through concrete; it's ruthless, but it's evolution. So if we cause pain to someone else in the process of our growth, well, that's just too bad, that's the nature of the beast. Life's got to happen, painful or not. And point number two—well, that was pretty much all the point I needed to make right there. . . . Ordinarily I'd've had Hilly, you know, proofread the pages first, maybe make a suggestion here or there, but since she's on my permanent shit list—

(Because no matter how sad she looks, or mad or mopey or depressed or whatever she is without her journal, that's just too bad, she should have fucking well thought twice before she stabbed me in the back like that. Pilot to copilot, every man for himself, right, Spooky? No matter how much it hurts.)

—I just did my own editing. But you can only see so far from your own perspective, I mean, a writer's got to have a reader, right? So I'm hoping for, I'm *expecting*, some positive input from Malcolm. Been expecting.

Because he's not living up to his side of the deal, is he? Not remotely. We haven't even discussed the pages I've already turned in, he hasn't told me what his editor thinks, how much more I need to write, any of that stuff. Really essential stuff. I mean, if I'm doing this book I need to know all that, right?

And I *am* doing this book. I have to, I— To show her. To make it worth it. It *is* worth it. Even for her. Someday.

But when I press Malcolm he gets all, what, impatient?

annoyed? What the hell is wrong now? We're collaborating, we're sharing the creative tension, so he doesn't have
to act like, like I'm some kind of imposition, some kind of
tedious tagalong pain-in-the-ass—

"—problem," Malcolm is saying. He sighs, a thin wind;
he clicks his laptop to sleep. "You can give me more pages
now if you want, but I don't know when I'll have the time
to read through them."

This is a disappointment, to put it mildly, this is bor-
dering on a fucking insult, but you act on the situation,
right, you don't let it act on you. And I can be mature, I
can wait. For a little while longer. "Well, when's the deadline anyway? When does your editor want to see my
stuff?"

He looks at me. Just—looks. "The thing is, I can't meet
with you anymore, Ivan, I don't have time right now. In
the fall, perhaps."

Perhaps? in the fall? and "What do you mean, the fall?
What am I supposed to do, just write all summer with no
one to, with no— What do you mean, the fall? When's
this book coming out anyway?"

He sighs again, a hiss this time. "I have a great deal of
work to do with Hilly's journal. I have to reconfigure it,
reformat all the entries, cross-reference with my own
notes—"

"Well I can do that for you, I'm the one who—"

"I don't really need you, Ivan."

I don't really need you, what the fuck kind of remark is

that? What is going on here? He's still looking at me. "Well then, I— My pages—"

"Just leave them with me. I'll get to them when I get a chance."

"I don't think so." My voice sounds weird, tinny, I force it down, I force myself up and "Give it back," I say, leaning over the desk, smooth dark slab, altar, my hands make moist marks on the wood. "My pages, the, the journal, all of it. If you don't want me you can't have— you—"

"No."

"I *said*, give me back the fucking journal!"

"No."

He's still looking at me, not mad, just looking, but all at once I, I just—lose it. I don't mean to, I wanted to discuss it all calmly, to analyze this ridiculous and stupid rejection, but instead I just start yelling, I push over the red-backed chair and "Give it to me!" bellowing, I feel like a bull but it comes out like a, a kid, a brat, a baby throwing a tantrum, which just makes me madder, I can't believe this shit is even *happening*, I can't believe he's saying—

"Calm down, Jeffrey. Just calm down."

What?

"There's no need to act out this way. You've certainly helped me with the book, and I'm pleased that—"

"*What* did you call me?"

"Excuse me? —Oh. Did I say Jeffrey?" He's sort of

smiling, this tiny sideways smile, clinking his bracelet. "I must have picked it up from Hilly. It's what she calls you, you know."

And I just— I stand there, I just *stand* there because I know, I fucking totally *know* that this isn't true, in a hundred million years Hilly would never do that to me. Never. She knows how much I hate that name, she—I might do it, maybe, if things were the other way around. But Hilly never would.

Jeffrey.

And I stare at him, I feel myself stare, gaze glazed like underwater, drowning, as he just watches and smiles. Like it's a show. Or a fencing tournament, the way you watch someone go down, you see his mistakes while he's making them, and you laugh to yourself: I'd never do that, you say, secure on the sidelines. I'd see it coming a mile away, I'd parry, I'd—

"Are you all right, Ivan? Are you—"

"I'm fine." That tinny voice again. I have to move, to get out of here, I have to go—and just like that I'm out of the chair, pages tight in my hand, because I just. Have. To go.

Out to the hall, the elevator, the parking lot, out to my car, turn the key and get going, get out of here, go home—

No.

Not home.

I put my head on the steering wheel, close my eyes against the sun, sharp morning sun beating through the windshield, too much light. Sweat on my cheeks. I turn the ignition off.

I can't go home. Cannot. Not to Hilly. Not now.

Jeffrey.

Oh my God, what a fuckup.

When I can, as soon as I can, I sit up straight, I wipe my eyes, I wipe the steering wheel. The black Mercedes, two spaces down, gleams like a bullet in the sun. Another car pulls in, a sporty little red BMW: it's Merry the receptionist, looking pinched and pissed. She glances but doesn't see me, slams her door, trudges inside.

Once she's gone I start the car again and pull out, carefully, slowly, drawing no attention to myself, just merging into the morning traffic, heading for the freeway. Go west, young man. Go west and keep going, until you don't have to think about it anymore.

I turn on XRZ; I light a cigarette. It tastes like heat, like nothing at all.

24

ADA WAS AN UTTER WRECK, THE WORST I'VE EVER
seen her. She kept calling Dr. Roland's office, twice, four
times, five times; were they sure Ivan hadn't said where he
was going, or when he might be back? No hint, clue,
joke, his jokes were often very subtle . . . no? Were they
absolutely sure, were they positive?

Then she called Grandma Kitty, which was the mistake
it always is. Then she picked up the phone again, to call
the police, Missing Persons, but Marshall said no, it had
barely been forty-eight hours, and Ivan would be furious
if we did that, so furious that he might not come home at
all. And then Ada cried, these huge, sick sobs, like her
body was turning inside out. . . . I remember watching
her and thinking, Would she cry like that for me if I were
missing? Maybe. But they love you more, they always
have. I don't really mind. Because I do, too.

And still they kept asking me, as if I might somehow
give a different answer if they asked long enough: Was I
sure I didn't know where you might have gone? Was I positive? Wouldn't I please, please tell them if I did?

Yes, I said. Because I was so afraid, I couldn't even really feel bad for them; my fear was like the ocean, limitless, bottomless, like one of those undersea trenches that go on forever. The Marianas Trench. The Hillary Fault. *Of course I'd tell you. But I don't know where he is.*

I'm going away for a while. Don't worry, that was all your message said. But it wasn't the message that was scary, it was your voice, that weird flat calm; you didn't sound anything like yourself at all. You might take off, you'd done it before: go stay in a hotel for a night, run up a big room-service bill, then zip home the next morning to laugh at us for freaking out over nothing. But this was different.

Monday morning: Wednesday afternoon. I remember sitting down with a map, state map from Marshall's glove box, and thinking, He could be anywhere. Anywhere. What was it, what drove him away?

Did I know? I think so.

I want to go in, I said. *To see Dr. Roland.* To find out what he did to you, because of course it was him, who else?

Maybe you can ask the doctor, Marshall said. *Maybe he'll have remembered something.* Ada didn't say anything; Ada couldn't talk. She just squeezed my hand before we left.

All the way Marshall drove much too slowly, kept the radio on too low: the all-news station, an endless stream of bad tidings, earthquake, house fire, outbreak, indictment. I just sat there, numb, folding and refolding the pages in my lap, why had I even written them? Habit? Because I had to write something? Because the false journal had somehow turned into the real one, another kind of backward writing. . . . In the cave I counted backward from one hundred to one, over and over, to keep myself from crying, from panicking. I did it then too, in the car, watching the traffic lights, the buildings go by, but all like a slipstream, like a tunnel; tunnel vision. Getting darker. Going down.

In hell Persephone weighs the pomegranate in her hand. Did she panic? Think what might have happened if she'd never eaten those seeds.

Persephone climbs through the caves. They are endless, and endlessly dark. Still she keeps on, stumbling, crawling, moving. Above, Ceres ceaselessly searches the earth, she whips her dragon chariot, she climbs to Olympus to confront Zeus and all the gods. She knows that love is the only thing that can bring her daughter back. Even when she learns the truth, that Persephone has foolishly eaten the pomegranate seeds, that she can never return all the way, still Ceres loves.

Persephone might have saved herself. But she didn't know how. Confusion is a darkness of the mind. Have you ever been all alone in the dark?

Love brings us back.

Marshall had to be told what turns to make, which floor the office was on. He walked down the hall like a robot, like he was blind. When we got to the door, RIVERSIDE ASSOCIATES, he paused.

Do you want me to come in with you?

No, I said, I'm OK.

Merry was on the phone; as soon as she saw me, she waved me inside. The hall reeked of lemon. His desk was covered with papers, forms, folders. I sat down hard, as if my legs were weak, as if I couldn't stand up any longer.

Where's my brother? I said. My voice sounded very small. *Where did he go?*

I've already spoken to your parents, Dr. Roland said. The sun made bars on the wall, on his crowded desk, on his folded hands. *Ivan didn't tell me he was leaving. He was somewhat upset. . . . Are you upset?*

I didn't answer. I picked hard at my thumb.

Are those pages for me?

No, I said. They're for me.

We haven't discussed your journal yet, but I have to tell you, I'm impressed. The pages about your friend, Elisha, about her suicide— they're very powerful.

"Discussed" my journal. Like discussing a rape. It was a rape. But he was still talking, about Ivan again: *Ivan did us both a favor, by providing this journal. I think without meaning to, he—*

He didn't do it on his own, I know that. You tricked him.

You know that's not true. In fact, it was his idea in the first place. Like Persephone, nodding at the pages on my lap. *Persephone and the pomegranate. No one force-fed her, she ate it because she was hungry. You might not want to believe it, Hilly, but no one forced Ivan to do anything.*

Persephone only ate half, I said. The fear was singing through me, a hard high whine, like someone crying in my ear. Fear and something else. *And she comes back. She keeps on coming back—*

Persephone, he said, just keeps going down. And I realized, he's enjoying this. Like you always enjoyed your fencing matches, the minute you were sure you would win. Going down eternally. But you can learn a lot, underground.

Clink-clink. My thumb was bleeding like fresh meat. The room was the cave. You tricked him, you sucked him in like a, like a mirror. My voice was smaller still, a little girl's voice. But not me. I can see you.

And what do you see, Spooky?

What do I see?

That smile. Elisha on the roof, barefoot, staring out into empty darkness. You, crying in the cave. . . . His tailored suit, like a mannequin's in a store; the cool showcase gleam of his bracelet. Merry's whisper in the waiting room: Give him nothing—

—and just like that, like a key in a lock, a mask removed, I did see: I saw him. Not eminent powerful Dr. Roland, not "Malcolm," but him. What there was behind the mask.

And as soon as I saw that, the fear just . . . just fell away. Like the guide lifting me out of the hole: I had been trapped, now I was free. Simple as that. The whole room seemed to open up, I sat up straighter, I think I even smiled as Nothing, I said. My voice was trembly with relief. I see nothing.

He stopped playing with his bracelet. His face was perfectly blank, like a bank vault, a smooth steel door.

You're nothing, I said. All you can do is talk in circles and confuse people who don't know any better. Like my brother.

Then he gave me a look I'd never seen before: the hunger. The real thing. Like a sucking chest wound. Or a starving mouth.

Your brother, that mouth said. Jeffrey.

His name is Ivan.

His name is Jeffrey. And he's gone, he's not coming back. Because of what you did to him.

Ceres. Orpheus. The guide in the cave.

You don't know that, I said.

Why did you tell me his real name? Did you want to humiliate him? That's very cruel. Did you know that you were cruel, Hilly?

I didn't answer; I didn't have to. In fencing they call it "disengage," right? when you fool the opponent's parry, you change the angle of the fight, and your blade goes free. When I didn't speak he changed course and got louder, something about the book, but there wasn't going to be any book, and I knew it. He probably knew it, too.

He was still talking when I picked up my pages and walked out. Disengage. I didn't even close the door behind me.

Merry was working, frowning, fingers clicking swiftly on the keys, but as I passed her desk she looked at me, a sharp look, eyebrows up; and I smiled at her. I felt so light, as if I were weightless, as if I could take two steps and fly. From the relief, I guess. Every cave comes to an end.

In the waiting room Johanna sat chewing gum and digging through her black saddlebag purse. Two chairs down, Marshall hunched over a travel magazine: couples scampering through the surf, a laughing child on a Ferris wheel: "Find Your Dream Destination!" He dropped it as soon as I walked out, a jerking motion, like the door was attached to his fingers.

We can go home now, I said.

Are you— What about Ivan? Does the doctor know where—

When she heard the name, Johanna looked up; I squeezed Marshall's hand. *Let's talk in the car, OK?*

OK, he said, confused; he squeezed back. He looked so old, old and exhausted and lost. Poor Marshall.

But we did talk, all the way home. Maybe it was the relief, all that clean air blowing through my brain, that made it easy. Maybe— I'm not sure what it was. But I was able to tell him all kinds of things, things about Dr. Roland, about his book, and my journal; things about you.

He even let me drive. I was careful in the traffic, the long turn onto Oak, past the busy car wash, the shiny green avenue of trees, careful as I pulled into our driveway, close up behind Ada's car, leaving your parking space empty. It looked so lonely, that vacant, waiting space.

He'll come back, I said. *I'm sure he will.*

Is that what Dr. Roland thinks? Marshall asked. His voice was hard.

That's what I think.

He put his hand to his face, scrubbed at his forehead, as if he was trying to rub away a thought. *We need to talk to your mother.* The car was hot; neither of us moved to get out.

Hilly, my God. Why didn't you tell us before? About Ivan and your journal?

Because it was between me and you. Because it was already too late. Because it was up to me. . . . But I didn't say any of that. Instead I put my hand on his shoulder, just for a second, and *I'm sorry, Dad,* I said, which was every bit as true.

25

NINE A.M. SUN ON THE BACK OF MY NECK, CHAR-
coal shadows growing from the slats of the bench; I've
been reading a lot about narcissism lately. Did you know
it's an actual psychological disorder? which is really kind
of ironic, considering Malcolm is a shrink. Physician, heal
thy fucking self. . . . It's from another Greek myth, perfect-
looking Narcissus leaning over the water, falling in love
with his own reflection. No one can measure up to what
he sees, so he just stays there, pines away for himself, and
dies. And behind him is Echo, the girl who loves him;
Echo, who always gets the last word. . . . I get the symbol-
ism, yeah.

The narcissist is fundamentally isolated, and becomes more so.
Choice by minor choice, decision by daily decision, others are forced
to the periphery. Ultimately, there is nothing left in the self's universe
but the self.

I light a cigarette, my third this morning, to go with
the last of the coffee; I'm seriously trying to cut down
smoking. Plus I'm getting really sick of street people trying to bum cigarettes off me; every time they see you fire
one up, they're swarming all over you, like it's downtown

Calcutta or something. Which is why they're called bums, I suppose.

This isolation becomes oppressive over time. But the price for escaping it is often too great for the narcissist to pay. The healthy person seeks connection, continues to reach outward, as he or she grows. And this growth inevitably involves a surrender of the self, a redrawing of the heart's boundaries to include the needs and wants of others. Most narcissists, the book says, simply won't do this. They'd rather live and die alone in their own heads.

I found this book in a thrift shop. There's a pretty good one down at St. Astrid's, right by the day-old bakery, that whole down-and-out district. They've got all kinds of novels, scuffed-up art books, textbooks, the kinds of things I'd be reading if I was in college right now. . . . They have clothes at St. Astrid's, too. That's where I got this shirt, and that red windbreaker thing I use for a coat. I'm trying to be very cool about money, you know, until I can get a real job. Right now I'm working at a convenience store, but mostly I'm living off Marshall and Ada's Visa. They said it was OK, to use it as long as I needed to, but still it's a, a link. To them. To home.

To Hilly.

I think about her all the time. At first it was just questions, like, is she OK? Is she still writing? Is she tarping out in the backyard again? Is she still seeing Mal—Dr. Roland? although I didn't really think so, I figured that without me to keep it going, Hilly would stop the whole show. And she did. Marshall told me. She told them all about him, and that was that.

Now I think about, you know, just about her. About telling her things, things I've seen since I've been here, stuff I've done. The way it is at the hostel, the industrial-strength bunk beds, the little scuffed lime-green lockers, the way it feels to sleep surrounded by strangers. What it's like to sit on a bench and watch people go by, a different bench every day but all of them the same. Sometimes I pretend she's there anyway, and make up a little dialogue in my head, I say this and she says that. But after about ten minutes it gets so depressing that I have to quit.

And I think about what she might be writing. What she might be thinking. And if she's maybe, you know. Mad at me.

I think about going home, too. Not like now, in the fresh-air mornings, or at night when I take my walks, but in the endless boring lonely afternoons, the hours and hours with no one to talk to, with nothing to do but smoke and read and smoke some more. Then I think about packing up my stuff—what there is of it; you'd be surprised at how little you can get by with; I was surprised anyway—and climbing in the car. It's not that long a drive, I could be there in a day. Turning down Oak, pulling up into our driveway—

It's not that I don't want to go back, to see her. Jesus, I do. But eventually we'd have to talk about, you know, things. And I just—I can't do that, OK? I can't stand there like an idiot, like a stupid mumbling Jeffrey jerk—

—but then, isn't it more stupid to keep on the way I am, keep pretending I just, what? suddenly needed to be

four hundred miles away? Like Dr. Roland kept pretending, trying to pretend, when I knew he was lying about
Hilly, lying right to my face. And smiling, like I was too
dumb to tell the difference, grinning away as he fed me
this giant fucking filthy deliberate lie—

—but if that was a lie, what else was? What *wasn't?*

He doesn't want you, Ivan, he's just using you to get at me!

He's not "bad," stupid. He's the smartest person I've ever met in
my life.

Which would mean I was— And she was right. About
him, about the book. About all of it.

The narcissist will go to any lengths to avoid confronting his own
emptiness, even if it causes pain to others. The greatest threat is self-
exposure.

It's not that I was, you know, mistaken about Dr.
Roland. Once I saw clearly what was going on, I acted, I—
Did you know that one quote, the one I really liked, is actually from Samuel Butler? "I don't mind lying, but I hate
inaccuracy." It's from his *Note-Books.* Dr. Roland just plagia-
rized it; another lie. Shuck upon shuck upon shuck. Like a
house of cards made out of razors.

He was so fucking *good* at it, though, you have to admit
he was good at it. The art, the girls, the books, the office,
the way he talked to me: confident, confidential, like there
was a secret, a mystery, some amazing essential knowledge
that he had and you wanted. And the closer you got to
him, the closer you got to it. That's how he made it seem.
Until you got right down inside it, all the way down to
the bottom. The way Hilly did.

But how did she know, right from the very beginning? She never trusted him. Not for a second.

I talk to Ada on the phone fairly regularly. She's always got a million questions, all her usual anxious-mom stuff, like what am I eating? where am I sleeping? are the street people trying to take advantage of me? (Fast food and day-old doughnuts; the hostel; and, except for the cigarettes, no.) Marshall and I talk sometimes, too. He's the one who asks what I'm doing, what I'm reading, what do I think of this or that in the news. Current events.

And they both ask, always, if I want to talk to Hilly, but I always say no. Pilot to copilot. Pilot to pilot. . . . Spooky, I didn't mean it, OK? And I'm totally fucking sorry, about your journal, and the tarp, and—everything. Everything.

Just please don't ask me to come home.

26

IN A WAY, I WISH I COULD HAVE GONE BACK TO THE office one more time, just to tell Merry what happened, that I knew how it really was with Dr. Roland, that I was OK. That I gave him nothing. But Marshall and Ada were completely against it. With you gone, it was like a spell was broken, or— I don't mean it like that, but you know how they are. Without you, they followed my lead instead. Which was fine with me. I wasn't afraid anymore, but that didn't mean I wanted to go near Dr. Roland ever again.

And once they heard the whole story, or as much as I could tell them, they just kept going over and over it, asking me the same questions again and again, like they couldn't believe what they were hearing: *But Ivan said the book was to help you, to get you writing again. He said that was why Dr. Roland was doing it. Why he was doing it. Wasn't that true?*

Yes and no, I said. Because the pages did help me, writing it all down, feeling my way through the dark. Not that Dr. Roland ever intended that. Just like you never really intended me to be . . . hurt. Like in the cave. Don't you think I know that?

They got my journal back, although I'm sure Dr. Roland kept a copy, even if he can never use it in a book— he needs permission, just like Merry said. Ada gave it to me, and I stuck it in a drawer. I don't want to look at it now, or maybe ever. Maybe never. Every time I see the cover, I think, *rape*.

They even asked me if I wanted a new shrink, someone who could really help me. *There are good ones out there*, Ada said. *Even some great ones*, Marshall said. So did I want to try again? because they would make it happen, they would do exhaustive research, they would do everything they could to make sure that things went right this time.

No thanks, I told them. *I'm OK*.

Marshall wrote this scathing letter to the state board, the shrink-licensing board. I helped him write it, even though I didn't think it would do any good, or do anything at all, really. Look at the facts: We make a complaint, *malpractice, malfeasance*, and Dr. Roland, what? Points out— kindly, rationally, even half-truthfully—that I'm a disgruntled ex-patient with a runaway brother and a history of hiding under plastic tarps. Who's going to believe me over him? or Marshall and Ada either, the semi-useless parents of semi-nutty kids? For a while Marshall was even muttering about getting a lawyer, but Ada and I talked him out of it.

Lawyers won't solve anything, Ada said.

Lawyers won't bring Ivan back, I said.

They talk on the phone to you once a week, almost; you're doing all right, they say. They say that you sleep at

a youth hostel, that you're trying really hard to quit smoking, that you got a job in a convenience store. I can just
picture it: You leaning sternly over the counter, grilling
some nervous twelve-year-old, *Are you sure you're old enough
to buy those cigarettes?* And you walking around the city,
noticing everything and everyone. Marshall said you told
him it's OK, mostly, but there's no one to talk to. I know
just what you mean.

If we could talk . . . you know, I have so many things to
tell you. Like for one thing, I can drive now. I went to
Roads Scholars and got my license. And I cut off my
draids; Ada helped me, and now my hair's all short and
smooth, like boot camp, you can see the curve of my
skull.

And I entered this poetry contest, *New American Voices*,
and my poem won an honorable mention. It was about
Persephone, and the tarp, and everything. When Ada read
it, she cried. I asked her if she'd send it to you, and she
said she would. Did you get it?

You still refuse to talk to me. But you did say I could
write you a letter.

So here's my letter, here's our book, Ivan. Just like
Otnarepse, I know you can read between the lines. If you
want, you can write the other half, tell your side of the
story. And after you do that, maybe then you'll be ready,
maybe then you'll decide to come home.

You know, I'm not mad at you, if that's what you think.
I was, before, but I know what it was like in that office,
the drawn blinds, the lemon smell: and Dr. Roland. Like

vacuum, sitting in a chair. It pulls at anything that comes near. No wonder it was always so hard to look at him. . . . Disengage, you did it too when you walked away, ran away, whatever. It was all we ever had to do, really. Just don't listen. And don't eat the seeds.

But even if you do—

See, in my experience, what's good always comes back; always. Like Persephone. Or Elisha. The guide in the cave. . . . Love brings us back. I said that in the poem, too, or tried to.

As soon as I see you, it'll be all right.

Untitled
    by Hillary Polo

Experience is a scar.
A muscle.
A rip in a blue plastic tarp.
Experience is Persephone, her mouth stained red
Like she's been eating glass.
The grass came back, where I sat so long
Alone in the yard.
Everything that lives, comes back.
Hell has a door.